MAGIC FLOWER POWERS

BY CHRISTINE BLYSTONE

Magic Flowers ©2023 by Christine Blystone
All rights reserved
Printed in the United States of America
For information, contact christine@velvetback.com

velvetback.com
literarykitchen.net

ISBN 978-1-950272-20-4

Illustrated by Christine Blystone and Ryan Newson
Cover and interior design by Christine Blystone

Set in Libre Baskerville and Floravian

First edition • 500 copies • Spring Equinox 2023

HELLEBORE

A winter goddess.

A respected elder.

A compass in the
Shadows.

"Embrace the
Still nothingness,"
She whispers,
"Allow your
Heartbeat to
Guide you back to
Your whole self."

THE WORM(HOLE) MOON

It was early springtime in Ponoka.

The time of year when the snow still clung to the ground, but the sun rose a little earlier over the prairie each morning. The time of year when the wind nipped everyone's ears less frequently, and Mary could walk to school each morning, her hands shoved into her grey wool coat pockets.

The hint of twilight in the sky kept her company.

It wouldn't be until the snow fully melted in April that she'd start spotting the wildflowers on the way to school. Harebells, Coltsfoot, and Wild Roses. They wouldn't be blooming quite yet, but she still knew them by their leaves' shapes, colors, and textures.

Mary thought about this while she walked the old, worn dirt path to school, breathing in the smell of woodsmoke that weaved itself through the ozone in the crisp air. The promise of flowers blooming always encouraged her on dark, chilly mornings.

With the light of the full moon shining down on her, Mary could see her breath sway in the air as she approached the log and sod one-room schoolhouse. The sign above the entrance read *Ponoka County Rural School*. At twelve, she was the oldest student in Miss Tansy's classroom.

She opened the door and stepped across the threshold.

Her fingers fumbled around in the dark until they found the soft cardboard box of matches sitting on the little wooden shelf just left of the doorway. She picked it up, opened the tiny paper drawer, took out a wooden matchstick, and struck it against the side of the box.

A quick blaze flared up at the end of the match. The strong scent of sulfur stung her nose. The wooden floorboards creaked under her as she quickly made her way around the room, lighting all the kerosene oil lamps on the shelves and tables before that first match could burn the tips of her fingers.

She took a moment to admire the warm orange glow illuminating the schoolhouse. She watched the dancing shadows cast folktales on the walls and listened to the wind trying to find its way inside.

She took a deep breath and felt her small body relax.

This was her favorite part of the day. A slice of time all to herself before Miss Tansy and the rest of the students arrived.

Her magic hour.

With the box of matches still in her hand, she approached the black cast-iron potbelly stove in the middle of the room. She knew this ritual by heart. First, she opened the big door on the front of the stove. After making sure the flue and the vent at the bottom of the furnace were open, she sat in front of the stove, legs tucked under her.

Every evening before leaving the classroom, Miss Tansy placed that day's newspaper on top of the crate of pine logs they burned for heat. Mary began crumpling the sheets of newsprint and, one by one, placed the paper orbs inside the stove.

Next, she took out her pocketknife from her right leather ankle boot, careful not to get any ink from the newspaper on her white cotton dress or freshly washed wool stockings. She picked up a log and began cutting kindling, stacking each shred of pine in a loose pyramid inside the stove. She struck another match and tossed it in, spreading the flame across the discarded paper stories. She packed in a few more logs, then paused before shutting the stove door.

The smell of woodsmoke and bubbling pine resin, sharp and sweet, swirled around her, and the crackling of the fire was comforting as it warmed her young face. As she stared into the hearth that morning, something new happened.

"Oh, my," she breathed, her pupils dilating. She tasted spit and salt and felt her heart thump. Exhilarated, she leaned into the experience and let go entirely as her consciousness traveled across the vast cosmos, a trail of rainbow prism light trailing behind her like a comet.

When her awareness returned to the room, she closed the stove door, stood up, and walked over to the little window by the door. The sun was just starting to rise on the other side of the schoolhouse, and she saw her reflection against the new morning sky. Her brown eyes stared back at her, and she took the time to braid her long wavy hair, securing the end with a lavender ribbon she kept in her pocket.

She never told anyone what she saw that morning after lighting the fire in that potbellied stove, but after that experience, she learned all she could about the stars, picking up any book she could find about astrophysics, astronomy, and astrology.

She studied math and science and wanted to know what else was out there in the universe. *Who* else was out there?

She dreamed of interdimensional space travel.

And she desperately longed to touch the soft dusty surface of the moon.

DAFFODIL

When life feels like
The grey storm of a
Never-ending winter

Soaking your
Downtrodden spirits
To the marrow

Daffodil illuminates
The path leading
You back to your
Inner flame.

A reminder of the
Magic it is to be
Alive at all.

When I was nineteen, and my hair was bleached and ragged like an aching sunset not ready to slip below the horizon, I found myself trapped in a cage, all life sucked from my marrow.

Dead inside.

I worked a shitty nine-to-five while my husband, Mark, gambled away all the money I earned. Most nights he'd wake me up in the small hours of the morning after he returned home from the casino and bark orders while he played loud video games. "I'm hungry. Make me a pizza."

I learned early on it was easier to comply than to say no. I'd rather be up for half an hour than get into a fight and not go back to sleep at all. Coarse, grainy particles of exhaustion stung my half-opened eyes. The smell of freezer burnt cheese and greasy pepperoni made my stomach turn. It reminded me how much nourishment was missing from my life.

Night after night, an immense sadness settled deeper into the sinewy threads wrapped around my heart. I'd slam the hot baking sheet on top of the stove, cut the pizza into slices with a big kitchen knife, then make my way back to bed. The never-ending sound of pixelated bullets ricocheting off the walls in our living room shredded what was left of my fried nerves as I closed my eyes and pulled my pillow over my ears.

Unrealistic expectations hung all over my body and pooled in the dark, hollow circles under my eyes.

"You're fat and the stretch marks on your belly are disgusting."

"You're so fucking stupid."

"What are you doing? Fuck up that drumbeat one more time, and I'll kick you out of the band and divorce you."

So many sharp, unloving words cut me and chipped away at what little self-worth I had left. I was boxed in so tightly, there was no room for even a splinter of joy.

Except for the baby. Nattie was the only thing worth living for. But I began to suspect Mark wasn't taking care of her while I was at work. The clear plastic bags of breast milk just kept piling up in the freezer.

That's when I began to pray.

Dear God, please take me in my sleep.

This was back when I still believed in a grey-haired oppressive father figure in the sky. A god who loved me only if I bought into the idea that love felt like gut-wrenching fear, and the only way to be accepted was to abandon myself completely and fill each decision with blind obedience. I'd fall asleep alone each night with hope in my heart that God would take pity on me and I wouldn't wake up. Instead, I began dreaming about daffodils.

While I slept, I became a bumble bee, flying from bright yellow bloom to bright yellow bloom, collecting pollen and feeling the sun on my face.

Another time I found myself walking down the sidewalk, stealing daffodils from strangers' yards and shoving them into my mouth, eating them as fast as I could.

I dreamed I was a tiny fairy, lost in a dark forest at night. I was terrified I'd be gobbled up by a great horned owl swooping in behind me until the crown of daffodils on my head illuminated the path to safety.

Every morning my eyes fluttered open to find the electric sunshine streaming into my window from the tall buildings across the street from my apartment.

I'm still here.

On one of these mornings, as reality began flooding back into focus, I looked down and saw the stitches and squares of calico that made up the blue and white quilt my auntie Jayne gave Mark and me for our wedding. Then the white walls of the bedroom came into focus, then everything else. Dirty clothes on the ugly beige carpet.

The open closet door stuffed with boxes of my belongings that I never unpacked from our last move. The baby's bassinet with the white quilted cover.

I shifted in bed and noticed my body felt different. Startled, I sat up and reached behind me, feeling as much as I could along my back and shoulders.

Were those... feathers?

I dragged my body to the bathroom. Flicked the light switch. The buzz of more electric sunshine radiated around me. I stared into the exhausted eyes that reflected back at me in the mirror. Then I slowly turned around and looked over my shoulder.

Shit. Where did these wings come from?

My wings spread open, and the rush of air hitting my face gave me a thrill I wasn't expecting, filling my chest with the metallic hiss of tiny yellow sparklers burning bright and warm inside me. Still in shock, I admired my new beautiful black feathers with wide eyes. The acidic glow shining down from the lightbulbs above the mirror did their beauty no justice.

These wings need to glide through the clouds.

I walked into Nattie's room and paused for a moment in the dark, watching her sleep in her crib. She was all tiny eyelashes and chubby cheeks.

Let's get the fuck out of here, baby.

I picked her up and held her close. I draped a blanket over her to keep her warm and safe. She sighed and laid her head down on my chest. I smelled the top of her head, her fine strands of baby hair so fresh and sweet.

I made my way down the hallway and when I reached the living room, I stopped when I noticed a picture hanging on the wall out of the corner of my eye, the glass smudged in its silver frame. I stared at the image of Mark and me from our wedding day, my young body draped in a long white dress. My lips painted red with Wet-n-Wild lipstick.

We got married two weeks after my high school graduation in the Christian church Mark's family attended in Portland, Oregon. Growing up in white American suburbia, I learned to believe in God through osmosis, even though my family never went to church. My parents grew up Catholic, and their experiences taught them churches were run by greedy hypocrites. "They'd only help people who could afford to put money in the collection basket each week. Everyone else was shit out of luck."

Looking at that photo of myself on my wedding day, I suddenly remembered what my best friend said to me when we had a moment alone right before the ceremony began.

"It's not too late. Don't marry Mark. Let's run away."

At the time, I laughed it off as a joke, but what would've happened if I'd taken her up on her offer? Instead, I'd walked down the aisle, and in front of everyone I knew, I promised to love, cherish and obey Mark until death do us part.

Well, I might as well be dead, so take this obedience and shove it up your ass.

I opened the big sliding glass door to the balcony. I looked out over the concrete at the Portland skyline. I loved this city. It took me too long to get here. I didn't want to leave, but I also couldn't stay.

Another time, city.

I took a deep breath in, stared up at the sky, and made a leap of faith for a better life.

My wings knew what to do.

As I flew away, I felt the wind and rain caress my shivering face.

The inky sky draped itself across my tired shoulders.

The ancient light beaming down from the stars permeated the heartache under my ribs.

And as I soared through the sky, I felt the greater web of the natural world envelop me with its gentle strength. I basked in that for as long as I could hold onto it.

My wings flew Nattie and me back to my parents' house across the river. We landed softly in the backyard, the thick green grass welcoming back my bare feet while the sunrise was just a whisper in the sky.

I was exhausted. Turns out, it's incredibly difficult to fly very far with brand new wings and a broken heart.

As my life came back into focus around me, a patch of yellow daffodils caught my eye.

I walked over, leaned in low, and really took in the details.

The raindrops clung to the bright yellow petals.
The delicate fringe in the centers and the strong green stalks supported each flower.

As I reached out to pick one, it lit up like a beacon. In that stream of light, I watched myself turn into a gorgeous raven, a black rabbit, a tawny owl. I saw myself playing in a band with other women and touring up and down the west coast. I saw the beautiful faces of friends and lovers I hadn't met yet. I saw myself going back to school. Twice. And I saw my hands writing and drawing in an old, spacious brick apartment back in the city.

In that moment, as I connected with Daffodil, I knew that despite the heavy load I carried, those yellow sparklers glowing inside my chest kept reminding me life would get better. It had to get better.

Daffodil said, "Never forget that you're the magic maker."

Things were hard.

They were about to get harder and heavier than I ever expected.

I looked down at my daughter, awake now, the universe sparkling in her eyes, a big grin on her face.

It would take her thirteen years before she'd grow her own wings.

I kissed the top of her head.

Time to learn some magic.

A RITUAL TO CONNECT WITH A PLANT ALLY

GATHER
- A plant or flower
- A notebook or journal
- A pen or pencil
- 10-15 minutes

Think about a plant you'd like to strike up a conversation with. Is this a plant in your yard? In your neighborhood park? Maybe it's your favorite house plant or a freshly-picked flower you brought into your home.

Find a relaxing place to hang out with this plant for the next ten minutes or so. Make sure you take the time you need to get comfortable before you begin.

When you're ready, close your eyes and take a deep breath, inhaling slowly and deeply into your belly. Hold your breath there for a few moments, then release. Go ahead and take two more deep breaths like this, and allow your breath to soften any areas in your body that might be tight or holding onto something from your day.

Now just spend the next few minutes hanging out with the plant. Be open to any messages you might receive, and jot down any impressions you get. Maybe you want to sketch the plant in your notebook or doodle to get into a creative flow. When you're ready, answer the following journal prompts:

What ten quick word associations come up when you think about this plant? *During this exercise, don't think too hard or judge what comes up. Just let the words bubble up from your mind and write them down. It's ok if some of them don't make sense at first.*

What healing truths are you receiving from this plant?

What is this plant trying to reveal to you about your own innate magic?

What feelings come up around the messages from this plant?

What are some ways you can bring the spirit of this plant into your life?

WINTER

I wanted my freedom, so I flew away.

But I didn't fly off into a summer of endless peach compote and rose elixir sunsets. Instead, winter kept stretching across the horizon. It was full of last season's wrinkled root vegetables rotting in the dusty root cellar. And sharp gorge winds carrying icy razorblades that pressed into the soft flesh of my neck.

I wanted my freedom, so I showed up in family court and protected my daughter, Nattie, as much as I could, even though a crusty old judge with thinning white hair and a jet black handlebar mustache told me that Mark—the person I was trying to protect her from—was allowed to see her every other weekend and on Wednesday evenings.

I instantly felt my heart shatter like a dropped mirror under the weight of it all.

Who was this asshole to tell me my 8-month-old baby would be ok with an abusive narcissist? Didn't he read the words **UNABLE TO RECOGNIZE THE NEEDS OF OTHERS** in the court-ordered psychological evaluation? Should I tell him that his Just For Men mustache wasn't fooling anyone? Or that I saw the fork in his lizard tongue when he licked his finger to turn the page on the parenting plan? Thick magma churned hot inside my belly and pooled into my shaking fists. Unable to erupt, it hardened into thick slabs of granite in my throat.

I couldn't breathe.

I wanted my freedom, so I showed back up to the ugly gray cubicle walls of my office job. I showed up even though my heart, now taped backed together haphazardly, ached every morning when I left my sweet-smelling baby with my mom so I could go work a job I hated. I pumped milk in the cold beige bathroom stalls on my breaks until my heart became so misshapen, the tape gave way and my body refused to produce milk altogether.

I wanted my freedom, so I showed up everywhere except for myself. So in some ways, things didn't change much, except that I didn't have to deal with an abuser all the time. I was getting more sleep, but I still wasn't living the life I wanted.

So while Nattie and I lived with my parents for over a year, I saved my money for a used 1998 Toyota Corolla. She was bright blue and I named her Betty. I convinced my friend Meredith she wanted to share an apartment with Nattie and me. And when my friend Wendy told me about grant money for single moms to go to college, I thought, *Huh. Maybe this will strengthen my wings and I'll fly greater distances. Maybe this is how I'll survive until spring.*

HOW I SURVIVED WINTER

Federal Pell Grants

Free childcare from my parents

My drumset (thanks to the divorce settlement)

Diet Dr. Pepper and Black Velvet whiskey

A Paragard copper IUD and condoms from Planned Parenthood

A pair of black knee-high boots from Payless Shoes

Jolenes band practice twice a week

My grandmother Mary's old radio on my dresser

AOL Instant Messenger

An Associate of Arts degree from Clark College

A RITUAL FOR SURVIVAL

Gather all your
Dark clouds of
Sorrow and the
Fibers of anguish
That descend like
Heavy, Glacial rain.

Bless them in the
Steely breeze as
They float away.

Amplify the light
Peeking through
The windowpane
Spilling joyfully
Onto the sill and
Enveloping your
Gentle heart.

GATHER
- A pinch of Thyme, dried or fresh
- A tealight candle
- A piece of paper to write a list on
- A pen or pencil
- 10-15 minutes

When you find yourself in a winter season of your life, it's time to make a list of things you need to help you survive.

Light your candle and set it down in a safe place it can sit while it burns. Let the light that emanates from it be a reminder that spring will eventually arrive.

Find a comfortable spot to sit and give your body a few moments of affectionate attention. A few ideas are:
- Taking a few deep breaths.
- Gently rubbing your shoulders, hands, or feet.
- Lightly stretching your arms side to side and over your head.

You know your body best. Whatever you choose to do, make sure it's something that feels good to your body and helps ground you into the present moment. If you're unsure, just ask your body what it would like and listen to the answer. Trust what you hear.

Set a timer for ten minutes and begin writing your list. I find it's always best to include a mix of practical and spiritual things. Remember that a few special treats and pleasures are essential to survival, too.

Don't worry or think about how you'll acquire these things. Just write them down. If something comes to mind that will help you survive but feels impossible to grasp, write it down anyway.

Once your list feels complete, read it over and pick one easy thing that you could work on gathering this week. Make a note of it or put it on your to-do list.

Sprinkle the thyme over your list and fold it into a pleasing shape. Place it in the bottom of your underwear drawer.

Before you blow out your candle, say, "I will survive."

Optional: Listen to Gloria Gaynor.

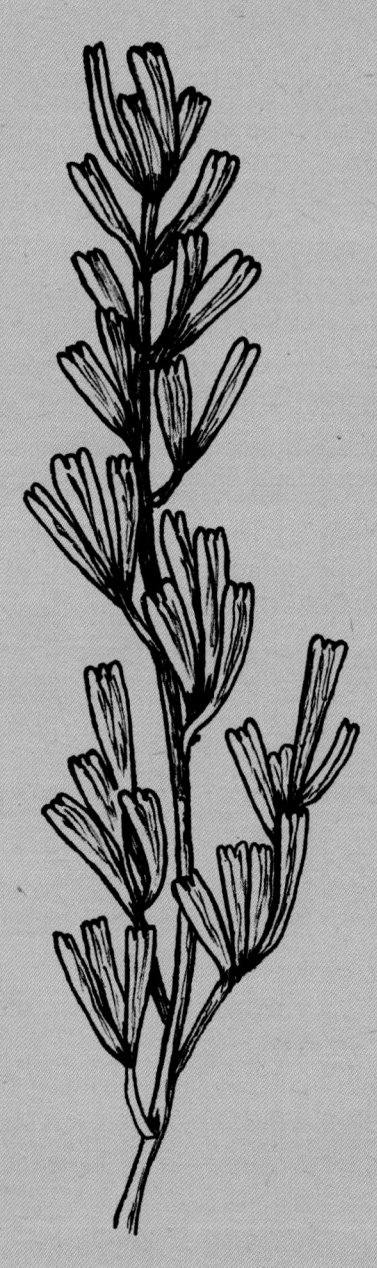

SAGEBRUSH

Wisdom
Heals the heart
And the spirit.

There is power
In clearing
The murkiness
To allow the
Sun in.

THE WOLF

Years later, when my hair was long and made of black raven wings, I began meditating. I'd lie on my back in bed, safe under the covers with my eyes closed, and gaze into the deep bronze sky of my eyelids. Focused on my breath, I'd pay attention to my belly rising and falling, and the whooshing air flowing in and out of my nose.

When my body relaxed and I felt soft inside, like a breeze meandering through a sunny meadow, my attention floated away. I found a thick wood hidden deep inside the folds of my mind and began wandering through the towering ancient trees. With each step, my feet sank into the paper-thin confetti of disintegrating evergreen needles that accumulated on the dirt paths.

In the middle of this seemingly boundless forest was an ancient giant redwood. The moment I saw the emerald green wooden door at the base of its broad trunk, I heard a slow, deep-throated rattle call from a raven that rang out gently from a nearby tree, as if to say, "You found your way. This is your quiet place to rest."

The room inside the giant tree was small and cozy. I squished my toes into the soft dirt floor, and felt a warmth wash over me, as I noticed an altar space where I could light candles and a soft bed for napping and dreaming. I took a few moments to stare at the golden sunlight streaming in through the little cutout window and watched the branches on the surrounding trees dance in the wind. I took a deep breath in, savoring the sweet and earthy smell of the bare redwood walls.

This place was safe.

I came here to escape the world when it was cruel, and life felt impossibly hard. I came here when I needed to still my mind and float away a little bit. It was my secret nobody else knew about. Where nobody else could be.

Until the wolf showed up.

One day, as soon as I entered my redwood temple, I felt a chill brush against my shoulders, and sensed another presence somewhere in the woods.

A dark figure was floating through the vast forest. She ran on all fours, but her feet didn't touch the ground. Charcoal smoke wafted from her strong, powerful body, curling around branches as she left grey streaks behind her ghoulish gait.

She was coming for me.

When I finally caught a glimpse of this creature circling just outside the window, the black pit in my stomach whispered, *'See? You can trust me. I'll always tell you when danger is near.'*

The wolf's keen ears must've heard the fear murmuring in my belly, because she looked up at me with her red, glowing eyes and my heart pounded against my ribcage. I saw the faint glint of sharp teeth in her mouth and a loud gasp escaped from my throat. I quickly opened my eyes and came back to the other side of reality. Safe in my bed.

Where did this wolf come from, and why was she after me?

A few days later, I went back to my giant tree, but the

wolf followed me there. I returned several times after that, but I was never alone. Haunted by this relentless ghoul, I became too frightened to return. So I went about my life and after a while, I completely forgot about that wolf and those beautiful evergreen woods.

Until the wolf showed up again.

I was traversing an angry red cloud that felt like an intense dust storm when I felt that familiar chill brush against my shoulders. And then I saw her emerge from the red smoke, her grey fur standing on end, ears pulled back, mouth snarling.

I stared at the wolf and wondered why she was so ferocious. So terrifying. So unrelenting. Even after all those years, she found me again through time and space. She didn't lunge at me like I feared she would. Instead, she just stood there, and we faced each other in a strange and distressing deadlock.

I felt the dark electric jolts of fear begin to swirl around in my belly and paid attention to how they traveled up and down my spine. As I started shaking uncontrollably, I kept watching the wolf as my fear washed over and through me.

The more I allowed my fear to flow freely throughout my body, the more it began to softly fade away. Instead of being trapped inside me, it found its way to my skin and I felt it evaporate into the air. As it left, massive blue waves of clarity washed over me.

I knew what I needed to do.

I had to reach out and touch this enraged creature.

I knew she wouldn't bite me. This wolf was me.

This wolf was everything I feared about myself. She was every part of me that I rejected, ridiculed, hated, and resented. Every shitty decision I felt guilty about. Every ugly secret I kept hidden so deeply. Every human need that I was told good people don't have.

This wolf was enraged because she was persecuted and misunderstood.

I knelt down and reached my now-steady hand out to the wolf. As soon as I touched the top of her head, she stopped growling and her ears popped up, facing my direction. The red smoky dust cloud began to dissipate. Her amber eyes became wise and kind, and the black smoke that once surrounded her vanished. Her fur smoothed back down along her spine, and her muscles relaxed.

I sat down on the ground and Wolf laid down next to me, her beautiful soft grey head resting on my lap. I put my arm around her animal body, which felt so familiar, and scratched behind her ears.

She spent her whole life fighting for this moment.

Suddenly we were in the high desert. The smell of petrichor and dust lingered in the air and we stood up to look over the horizon at the low rocky hills. Hex-breaking sagebrush and healing juniper shivered in the wind. Rain was coming. We could see the dark clouds racing across the desert sky. Wolf stood next to me, her soft body pressing against my leg.

"Let's go dance in the rain," I said to her.

She looked up at me with joy in her eyes.

We took off towards the clouds and when the large droplets began to fall on us, we danced and laughed and jumped over the mounds of fluorescent mint green rabbitbrush with its luminous yellow flowers until our hearts felt like they were beating out of our chests. I sat on the wet ground, Wolf next to me with her tail curled around her front feet, and I closed my eyes.

I listened to the rain hitting the earth all around me. It was coming harder now, the sound of every single droplet merging with the next until all I could hear was a peaceful, undulating soundwave as a wild sheet of water washed over me.

I smiled and tasted the relief of warm salty water rolling down my cheeks.

ROSEMARY

It wouldn't stop raining.

A curious crow sat on the ledge of a brick apartment building in Brooklyn, doing his best to stay dry. He puffed his feathers up, trying to keep warm, and looked out over the white and yellow glow of the city lights.

How long have I been here? he thought.

He moved to the big city years ago, tempted by what he read in magazines about endless shiny things and machines that excited his inquisitive mind. Those things were thrilling for a while, but life in the big city had become a real drag.

It wouldn't stop raining.

The curious crow sighed and when his breath expanded his belly fully, he smelled something that stopped him in his tracks. He looked over his left wing to find a small brown planter filled with Rosemary sitting behind him, big wet raindrops collecting on the tiny green leaves.

He hopped over to the planter and used his beak to snip off a fragrant sprig with a light snap. Now that the aroma enveloped him, he no longer found himself in New York.

Instead, he was flying over a tall mountain with a sharp peak covered in snow, surrounded by lush rainforest. Long strands of chartreuse moss hung down from craggy tree branches. Blue rivers flowed all around the mountain, telling old stories to the rhododendrons and bear grass.

The scene was such a vibrant, technicolor contrast to the drab concrete, dusty red bricks, and endless grind his city had to offer.

As the curious crow descended deeper into the forest, wings outstretched strong and free, he noticed a gorgeous owl perched in a tall Douglas Fir.

"Are you ready to come find me?" the owl asked, as the curious crow's black talons hooked onto a nearby branch to rest on.

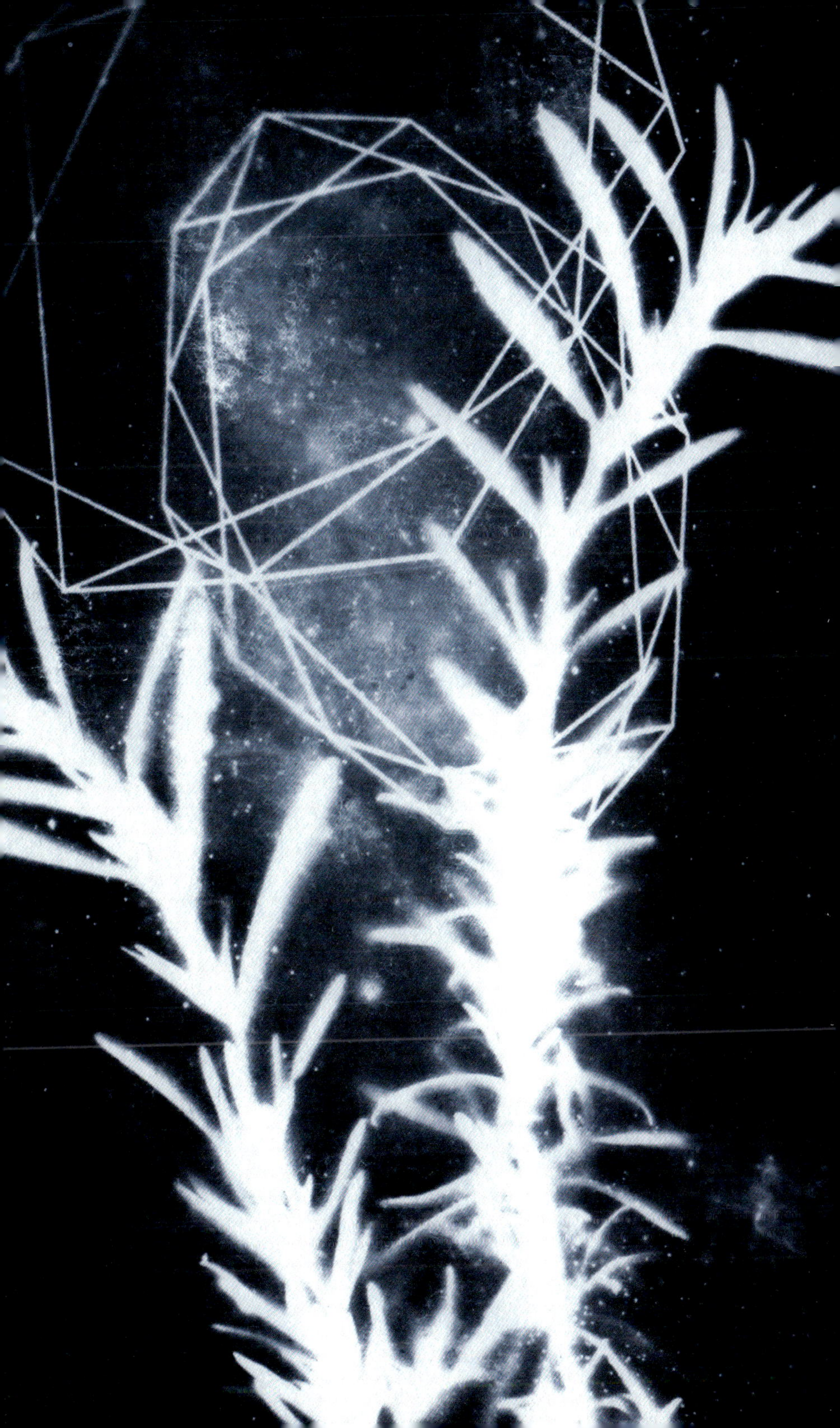

PHLOX

Feel the sun
Warm your face
And follow the wind
With wild abandon.

Jump into the
Freezing mountain
Waters of possibility
Invigorating your
Bright, fearless heart.

Explore the wilderness
In your unspoken dreams
And watch yourself
Blossom abundantly.

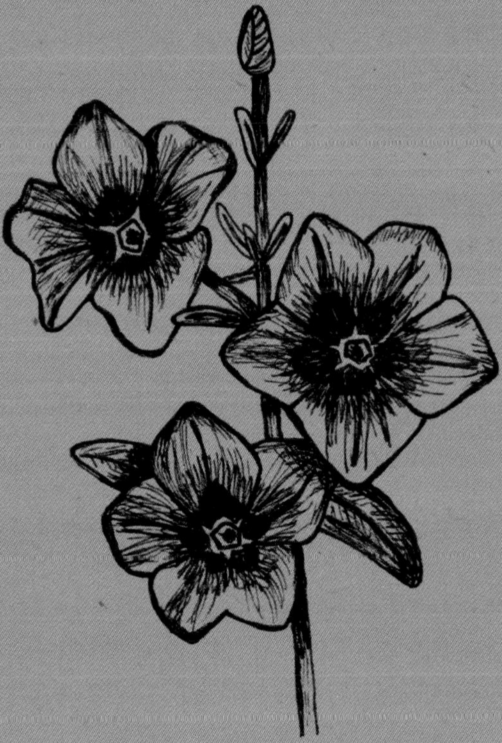

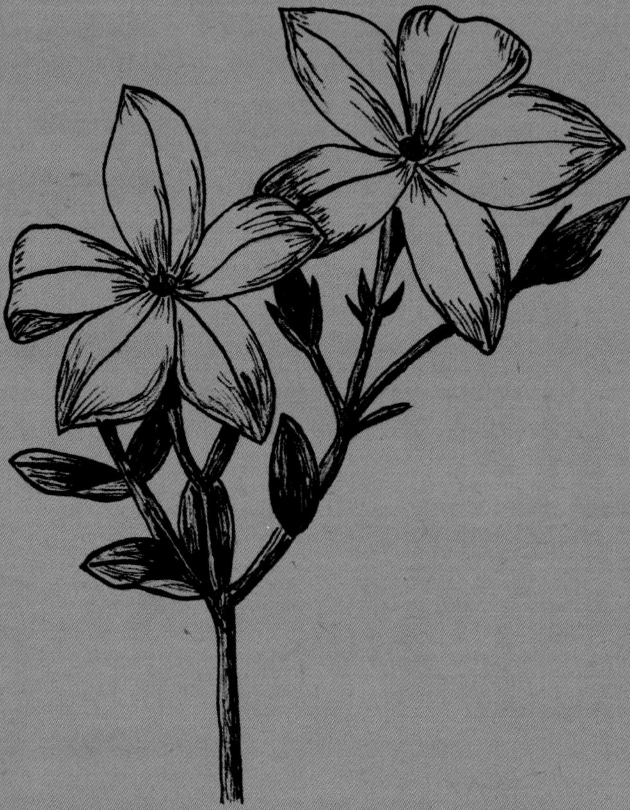

JASMINE

"I'm your German Shepherd," Jasmine would always say, and I loved it because I felt cared for and protected.

I met her on my first day back in college, in Matt Livengood's Intro to Communication Design classroom at Portland State University. She came floating in on a sharp autumn breeze, five minutes late, with perfectly straight bangs, ripped black tights, and her black mary janes from Payless Shoes levitating across the floor. I sat in the back of the room, where I felt comfortably unseen. She took the only empty seat, two tables in front of me.

I want to be friends with her.

I followed her outside during our fifteen-minute break.

"Hey, do you want to find some coffee with me?" I asked.

"Yeah, that sounds great," she said, adjusting her black bag on her right shoulder.

I smiled as we walked along the concrete sidewalk under the wet, silver sky until we found hot coffee in paper cups.

A soft glow followed us back to the classroom.

From then on, I saved her a seat next to me in the back of the room.

Once that first quarter of art school was over, I invited her to hang out with me over Christmas break. The spark of connection between us was effervescent, and I wanted an opportunity to get to know her better.

We both lived in the same NE Portland neighborhood, so we planned a date to walk across the Burnside bridge, eat Thai food, and sit on Santa's lap at the fancy mall downtown. Afterward, she invited me over to her apartment, and we sat on her bed and looked out her window over the clouds that wrapped themselves around the tall buildings across the river.

We became inseparable at school. Hanging out on campus. Meeting for lunch. Taking classes together. Drinking lots of coffee and talking on the phone. Everyone asked if we were sisters. We were both in our late twenties, heading towards our Saturn returns, with hazel eyes and long black plumage cascading down our backs. We lived in black hoodies and crisp winged L'oreal liquid eyeliner.

Loving Jasmine was easy. She was smart, funny, talented, and beautiful. Mysterious even. But what surprised me most was that loving Jasmine helped me love myself. We were so similar that I eventually realized all the things I loved about her were true about me, too.

She was my mirror. And I could see, for the first time why someone would want to love me.

We continued to get closer after we began our new lives after graduation.

During my divorce from the darkness, Jasmine was my rock. I drank vodka crans in my bathtub while I talked to her on the phone. She made me laugh and find strength. Humor and love just go together.

That same winter I smoked cannabis for the first time, sitting on her bed while we watched the clouds wrap themselves around the tall buildings across the river.

We listened to good music and talked about boys, art, work, and family. I always loved hearing her recount her latest documentary obsession.

We watched *Moonstruck* on VHS and drank perfumed green tea that tasted like soft, delicate flowers and good luck.

We dreamed of starting a goth band—me on drums and her on synth. I'd change my name to Jade. We almost rented a practice space from a dude whose name doesn't matter, and I can't recall anyway. All I remember is that he turned out to be a real creep, and when we ran into him at Club 21, Jasmine told him, "I will literally kill you," with a sinister smile, her sharp canines glinting like a sharp knife in the glow of the jukebox.

My German Shepherd.

We ate rare steaks and drank extra dirty martinis in that dark bar under the Morrison bridge. The hot, dingy summer air stuck to our bare arms and legs as we walked back to Jasmine's apartment.

"Oh my god. Last night I woke up around midnight and looked outside my window," Jasmine said, her voice low as she pointed up toward the sky, "Do you see that pole up there on the Lovecraft's roof?"

I saw the thick silver pole and nodded.

"Well, in the dark, it looked just like a shirtless Val Kilmer playing an electric guitar. I thought I was seeing some really racy shit."

We doubled over with laughter, savoring the peculiarity of life, and the comfortable familiarity of the airtight devotion between us.

We probably walked over a thousand miles together around those tall buildings across the river, building a friendship that eventually disappeared as quickly as it floated into class on that sharp autumn breeze, five minutes late.

I still dream about Jasmine and some psychedelic version of Portland that's been xeroxed and screen printed in unrecognizable ways across my mind.

In the dream, I walk by her old apartment and see her leaning out her third-story window. She looks down at me and motions for me to join her before disappearing back inside. The tingly rush of relief cascades down my head and slips out the tips of my toes. I make my way up all three flights of stairs and down the long fluorescent-lit hallway to her dusk colored front door. Just as I'm about to knock, I hear the click of the deadbolt unlocking and the door swings open on its squeaky worn hinges.

"Hey," she says, all nonchalant. She's wearing the black and white striped dress I gave her for her thirtieth birthday.

"Hi, Jasmine. It's...," I pause, struggling to find the right words, "... so good to see you."

I immediately feel embarrassed that's all I could manage to say.

I step inside and we both feel what's been left unsaid for years. It's so palpable, I'm scared it will take shape and swallow us whole. I feel awkward, but still so full of love for her. She's uncomfortable and doing her best to stay stoic, but I also sense there's still love for me somewhere inside her.

I follow her to her bedroom, and notice she still sleeps on her old futon. We find a hidden door made of thick wood tucked inside her closet. Her fluffy black and white cat, Bandit, circles around her legs. I crouch down to scratch behind his ears and he begins purring.

"Did you know this was here?" I ask.

"No," Jasmine grabs the brass doorknob. She tugs the door open and begins to walk into the darkness.

I get nervous and feel hot white electricity spark in my belly as my limbs tense up. I've never been good at trusting the unknown. I swallow hard, then follow her through the open doorway, squeezing my eyes shut tight as I take the first few steps.

I feel Bandit run past my legs.

The moon is bright and shines down from the endless shimmering night, casting shadows from the cypress grove onto the dusty dirt road in front of us. Luminous diamonds dot the sky. I look back to close the door behind me, but it never existed in the first place. The smell of sweet honey-scented flowers lingers in the air. All I hear is the peaceful hum of insects and the wind rustling through the branches.

We walk down the path in front of us, and I want to say

something before she disappears.

"I regret not fighting for you," I say. Soft blue light surrounds us, and the white stripes on Jasmine's dress glow pale turquoise.

She turns around.

"This life is just like that," she replies, looking into my eyes, "But there have been so many lives before this one and so many that will come later. Each time, we always find each other."

I take her hand before she can turn back around.

"I know," I say, "But it's still true."

She squeezes my hand and turns back towards the path. We begin walking again, and this time I'm beside her. Her hand is warm and familiar. I held this hand so many times at Beulahland and Virginia Cafe, the way you do when you have a best friend. We'd hold hands across the cheap laminate tables, and I'd make so many promises I meant in the moment, but couldn't keep later.

"The universe doesn't care," she says, "We came together for a brief moment to do something important and beautiful, and we succeeded." Jasmine looks over at me and smiles, and the moon turns her eyes into labradorite, rainbow streaks flashing in her pupils.

The insects hum in the pregnant pause.

"You're just remembering the parts you want to, anyway," she continues, "You know, the good times, and not any of the pain or frustration. As we got closer, I wanted you to be my mom, and you kind of wished you could be. But not really. You didn't need another kid to take care of. You needed a friend. In the end, neither of us could be what the other needed."

I know it's true. And also totally ok.

My German Shepherd.

The branches keep rustling as we continue taking one step after another.

A wry smile stretches quietly across my face as I remember a line from the first song we never finished writing together.

"My heart is breaking while yours evaporates," I recite, looking over at her beautiful face.

She laughs. "What the fuck did AIAK stand for anyway?"

I rummage around in my brain for the answer. I can't seem to find it. The last seven years without her have overwritten the name of our band.

"I'm pretty sure it was 'Actually I'm a Killer.' We were sad goths because we decided long ago that it would be fun."

She reaches up and touches the dark brown and silver feathers that frame my face.

"I remember when these were black and shiny like obsidian," she says.

"I'm an owl now," I nod, pointing to the flowering vine flecked with white blooms that stretches out beside us.

The sweet honey-scented petals glow in the moonlight.

Mystery. Love. Psychic dreams. Enchantment.

That was the contract we signed so long ago in the ether and fulfilled in the space where the jasmine blooms.

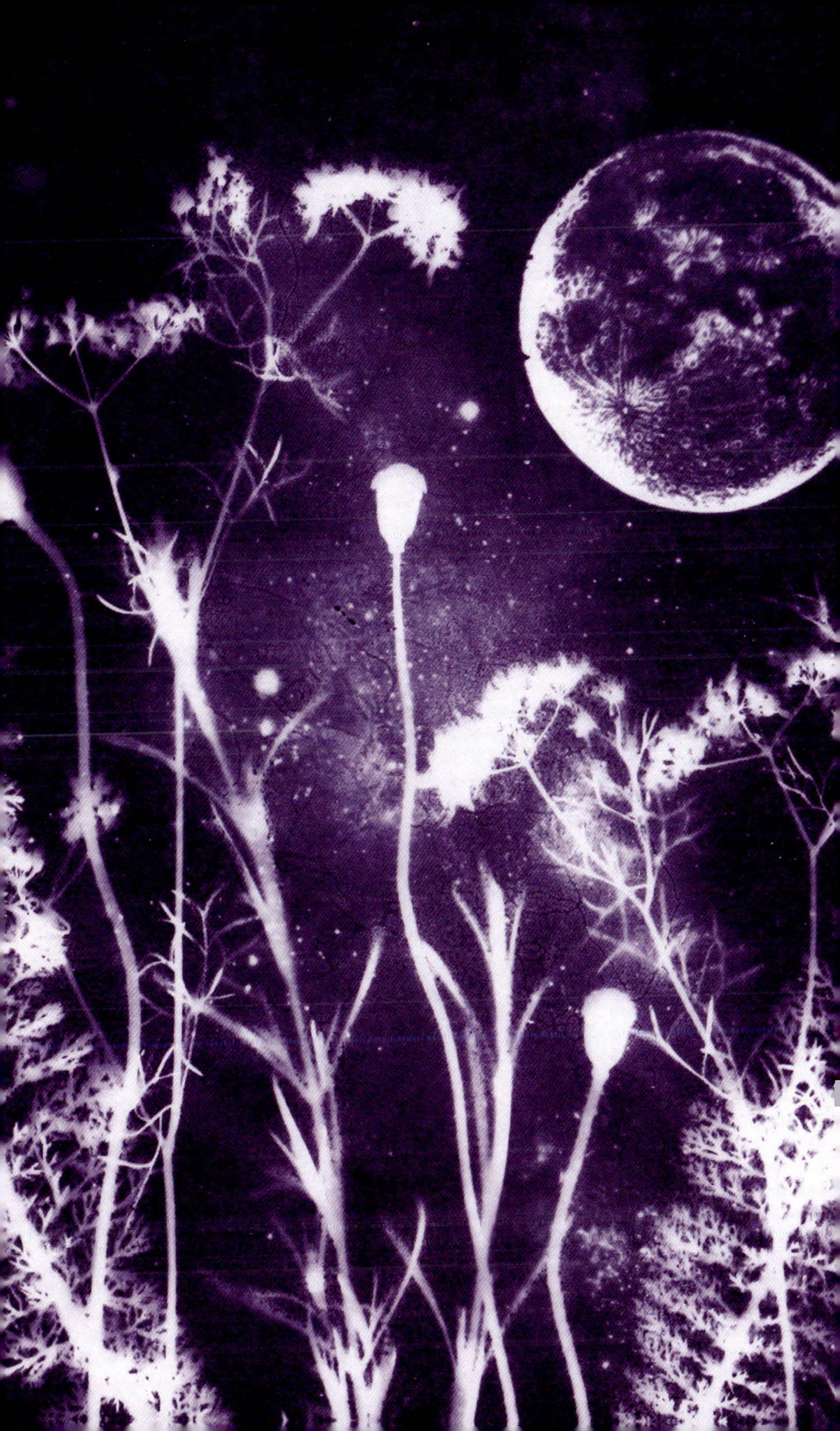

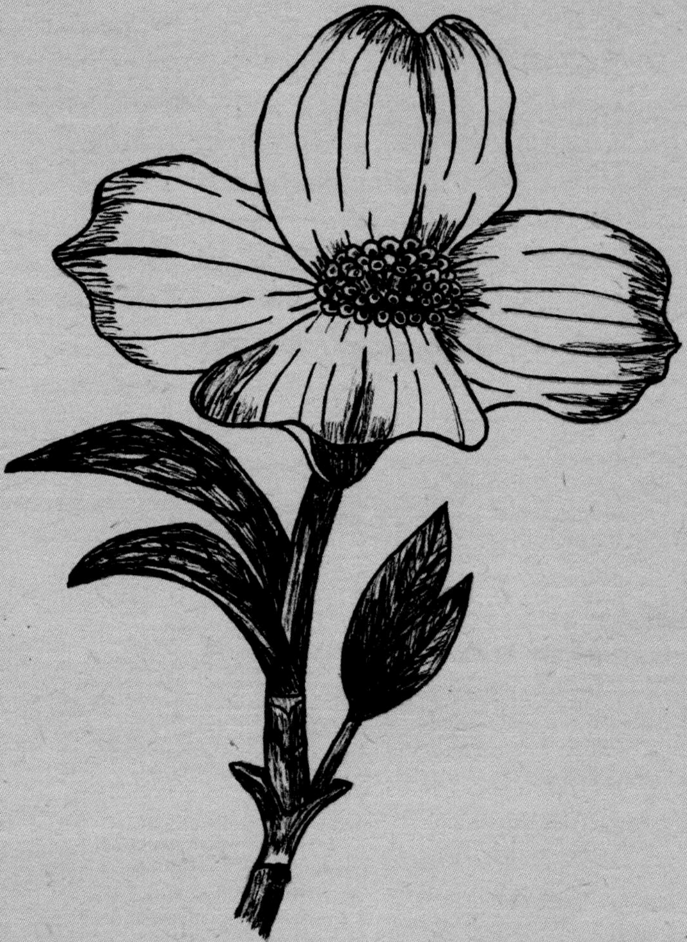

DOGWOOD

Ryan and I met at the end of my Saturn return at a greasy spoon dirty dive bar called My Father's Place on Grand Avenue. It's like Mel's Diner from that old seventies sitcom *Alice*, only darker, carpeted, and drenched in cheap booze.

While distracted and fucking off at my day job earlier that day, I discovered that the Crocodiles, who Jasmine and I had been listening to nonstop over the summer, were playing at Bunk Bar that night. Jasmine was returning to Portland that day from a short trip to visit her dad in Los Angeles, so I called her, hoping to catch her before her flight took off.

"I know you're ready to come home and eat sushi and take a hot bath and chill out, but please come out tonight. Just say yes, and I'll get our tickets to the show," I pleaded to her over the phone.

"I'd love to," she said, "I'm about to board my plane. I'll see you tonight."

When I arrived at Jasmine's apartment that evening, she said, "I invited Peter, Lia, and Ryan to meet us for food and drinks at MFP before the show—is that ok?"

"Yeah, of course," I said, as she motioned for me to sit on her old futon so we could hang out in her bedroom while she stood in front of the mirror on her closet door. She was in the middle of applying her black eyeliner.

I'd never met any of these folks before. I'd only heard

Jasmine tell a few stories about them.

I knew that Jasmine met Lia at Sheridan's, a grocery store where Lia worked as a cashier. They hit it off one day while Jasmine was buying a few cans of Progresso split pea soup and a cheap bottle of red wine.

"My band Il Marzo is playing a show this Saturday night," Lia said as she handed her a flyer for a house party, "You should come."

When Jasmine arrived that Saturday night with a few tall boys of Pabst Blue Ribbon to share, their friendship began to blossom. Lia and her boyfriend Peter lived up the street from Jasmine, and they all became quick, close friends over the summer.

That autumn, Peter's brother Ryan moved from Brooklyn to Portland to attend grad school. He was crashing with Peter and Lia for a while until he found his own place. Ryan was a drummer, just like me. This trio of strangers I was about to meet all played in Il Marzo together.

Ryan was the last to arrive at My Father's Place that night of the Crocodiles show. He came jaunting inside, the crisp mist of late autumn still clinging to his face, his tall frame nestled into his thick red and black plaid jacket. He took a seat across the table from me. When our eyes met, his kind blue eyes sparkled, and he smiled. He had chin-length light brown hair that was shaved on one side, and he looked pretty cute with his big beard.

"So you play in a band too?" Lia asked me, her intense dark eyes piercing mine. Her long dark coffee colored hair framed her face and cascaded down her vintage navy blue and tan houndstooth jacket. She was gorgeous like Jasmine, but in a punk rock hippie sort of way.

"Yeah," I said, "I play drums in the Secret Ceremony, but I used to play in a band called the Jolenes about a decade ago."

After we all had some drinks and shared a big pile of french fries, Jasmine convinced her friends to keep hanging out, and they joined us for the show that night at Bunk Bar.

When the lights dimmed and the Crocodiles took the stage, Jasmine and I grabbed hands and made our way to the front of the stage, where the air was hot and smelled of pungent body odor. But we wouldn't be deterred.

We screamed with delight when Brandon Welchez started playing the jangly guitar riffs of one of our favorite songs, Endless Flowers. I started moving my feet to the beat when the kick drum's reverberations sliced through my body in ways that reminded me of what it felt like to be alive.

I've waited here, waited my tears
On a crooked staircase with this melody

I looked over and saw Ryan standing next to me, dancing and bobbing his head while watching the band. The purple and green stage lights swirled around the room.

I can feel your heat through the television screen
I feel like I'm lost in space
Without your loving flowers to taste

He looked over at me and our eyes caught each other's gaze, tangled in the delicate threads of a tiny moment so familiar and exciting and sweet. Like it had happened in at least five lifetimes before.

All our endless flowers will grow
All our endless flowers will grow
All our endless flowers will grow
All our endless flowers will grow

When the band belted out the last song of their set, completely drenched in sweat and giving their all for the grand finale, the thick air and all the raucous energy of the club compounded, becoming the wide bands of dark clouds that hovered outside in the sky. Our little group finished our beers, left the bar, and started walking east, back towards Grand Avenue.

Walking down the sidewalk, I watched the silver drops of rain suddenly glow gold in the streetlights as I slipped my arm through Ryan's. Each drop that landed on my face and hair felt like a fresh start and a blessing. Years later, sitting around the warm orange glow of a campfire in the Tillamook State Forest, Lia would tell me, "Yeah, that night, he got home all twitterpated, sat down on the couch, and said, *'She's cute!'*"

Ryan and I had our first official date a week after the Crocodiles show. He invited Jasmine and me to a group art show he was a part of, and then we saw *Terminator 2* at the Bagdad Theater, where he and I held hands in the dark. Afterward, he walked me to my car, which was parked across the street from Sylvia's Psychic Insights, and we kissed in the rain, our faces framed by the enormous purple crystal ball neon sign hanging in the window. That night, instead of glowing gold, the raindrops glowed an amethyst hue and danced on our shoulders as they passed by us in the midnight wind.

A few days later, I sent Ryan a text.

Hey, do you want to go to Revival Drum Shop's flea market and eat lunch at Pattie's Home Plate Cafe with me?

Absolutely :)

Afterward, we walked around the old buildings and tall trees of St. Johns, getting to know each other more.

"I had a dream the other night that I was in a gorgeous tile soaking tub surrounded by windows that looked out into the forest," I said as cars whizzed by us on Lombard Avenue.

"I'd totally help you build a soaking tub," Ryan said.

"And help me pick out the plants to put around it?" I asked, recalling the potted monsteras and jade plants surrounding the tub in my dream.

Ryan raised his eyebrows and nodded, a big grin on his face. I began imagining us living out in the woods together, relaxing in an outdoor soaking tub we made ourselves, drinking vodka crans naked.

"Oooh! Look at those leaded glass windows," Ryan said, pointing up towards a gorgeous old brick building.

"I love those," I said, "They remind me of an apartment I used to live in across the river in Camas, Washington. Back when Nattie was so little. I really loved that place."

My favorite moments from those early days when Ryan and I were falling in love, though, were hanging out at my apartment in the evenings, making dinner for ourselves and Nattie. Ryan would bring in a paper grocery bag filled with olives, salmon, spinach, and red wine. There was so much ease between the three of us, lots of laughter, and it felt so light after enduring the darkness.

The darkness began creeping in about three years before Ryan and I met, and it slowly consumed every last bit of life out of everything around it. Toward the end, I spent months with a familiar black pit in my stomach, barely eating. It got so bad that all I could manage to eat each day was a bland vanilla protein shake for lunch.

The body never lies.

And neither do the trees.

The dogwood outside my dining room window stopped blooming when the darkness emerged, its magic dampened by the black hole just on the other side of the brick walls.

When I finally couldn't take it anymore, I slipped the moonstone ring off my left hand for the last time and spent weeks unearthing the darkness. I clipped back its thick, thorny brambles and dug out its rotten roots. Putrefied, they broke apart in my hands. There was so much fighting and crying as all the anguish, frustration, resentment and pain poured out of me. But by the time my hands were covered with black slime, I had no tears left. I was just desperate to be free.

"You're so cold," the darkness said, "You don't feel anything."

Those words hit me so hard that the black pit in my stomach enveloped me completely, and I sailed back in time. For a moment, while I stood there stunned and shaken by such a harsh blow, I remembered moving into my apartment that beautiful June day all those years ago, when I was just twenty-five. It played like an old movie in my mind.

I could see the pink blossoms of the dogwood tree outside my new dining room window, which were at their peak as the movers brought our boxes of belongings up the stairs. I watched as my younger self smiled as she admired the blooms, which were so bright, they were vibrating in the early summer sunshine, welcoming her home.

That new start felt like a lifetime ago.

I shook off this old memory and kept moving forward with my battle against the darkness. As I continued to excavate more decomposing branches from my apartment, the darkness tried to call me.

I swallowed hard and blocked its number. A warm wave of relief washed over me, and I let out the breath I'd been holding in so tightly.

Eventually, I removed everything—even all the dusty taproots that tried to hide under the hardwood floors. Then I salted the earth so it could never grow back.

When the darkness was finally gone, I looked at the sad dogwood outside my dining room window. The sun glimmered through its bare branches.

Fuck, we survived a season in hell, didn't we, dogwood?

So when I met Ryan for the first time at My Father's Place, I wasn't looking for anything serious. And neither was he.

He swore to himself that he wouldn't date anyone at all while he was in grad school, even though before he left New York, he had a vision of coming to Oregon and falling in love amongst the towering douglas firs.

In those early days when we were getting to know each other, we would snuggle into my twin bed most nights, talking well past two in the morning, even though we both had to get up early. We were so high on each other, it didn't matter. I floated to work each morning.

On one of those nights, tucked into each other's arms between conversations, we watched as the streetlamps outside created moving shadows across my empty bedroom walls.

"You've been through so much," Ryan said in awe, "But you didn't let it break you."

I felt my eyes fill with big, wet tears and the inside of my nostrils grew hot. At first, I tried to hold it back. A part of me didn't want to cry on this sweet man's chest. But there was no stopping it. My whole body began to shake.

With the darkness gone, there was room in my apartment for joy, laughter, and new adventures.

There was space for vulnerability and authenticity.

"Nope. I wouldn't let it break me," I said through the tears, and kept on crying and shaking.

Ryan hugged me tighter.

It felt so good to be held.

"You're amazing," he whispered.

That was our date that never really ended. With Nattie's approval and blessing, Ryan moved in a few months later, and the following spring, the dogwood outside our dining room window began blooming again, each petal bigger, more vibrant, and magical than ever before.

A RITUAL FOR A SAFE AND JOYFUL NEST

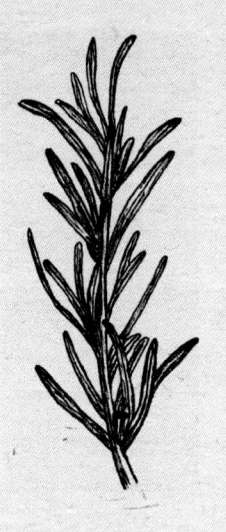

When your mind is
Full of squirrels
Or ghosts
Or an open
Sack of marbles
Rosemary is there
To shake the blankets.
Vacuum in one hand.
Sword in the other.
Clearing and cleaning
Then pulling the
Bed sheets tight.

GATHER
- Rosemary - either a handful of fresh sprigs or 2-3 Tbsp. dried
- Table salt - 1lb canister
- Enough small vessels for each room in your house. For this ritual, consider each closet a room, too. They don't need to be anything fancy. Ramekins, sauce cups, muffin papers, or any other tiny cups work well.
- A song that makes you feel empowered. Make sure that it's one you like singing or humming along to.
- A glass of water

Open all the windows in your home, as much as you are comfortable doing so. If it's just a crack, that's totally fine.

Play your song and make sure it's set on repeat.

Sit down and take a deep breath. Think about all that

you've been through this past season. Honor any feelings that come up by greeting them with a kind hello, and allowing them space to be there. Think about all the fresh air entering your home, ushering in a new era. A new beginning.

Start filling each vessel with table salt. Add a small sprig or a pinch of rosemary on top of each one. After you've filled all your vessels with salt and topped them with rosemary, walk around your home and place one in each room and closet. Pick out-of-the-way places where they can sit for a week, absorbing any stale, unwelcome energy from your home. When you are ready, close all your windows and let the song play one last time.

Seven days later, open all your windows and play your song on repeat again. This time, sing or hum along as you work. Dance or move joyfully if you feel like it. One by one, pick up each small vessel, and dump the salt, rosemary, and stale energy into the trash, taking care to pour everything out away from you, not toward you. When you're done, take the trash out of your home.

When you get back inside, wash your hands. For the next few moments, take some deep breaths with your eyes closed and come home to the present moment. When you feel your energy start to slow down and settle quietly inside your body, open your eyes, close all your windows, and let the song play one last time.

Pour yourself a glass of water, and sit down in your favorite place to rest. Think about all your hopes and dreams for the season ahead. Instead of writing them down, say them aloud into your glass of water. As you rest and drink, feel yourself absorbing your wishes and notice if you feel safe and lighter in the clear, fresh energy in your home.

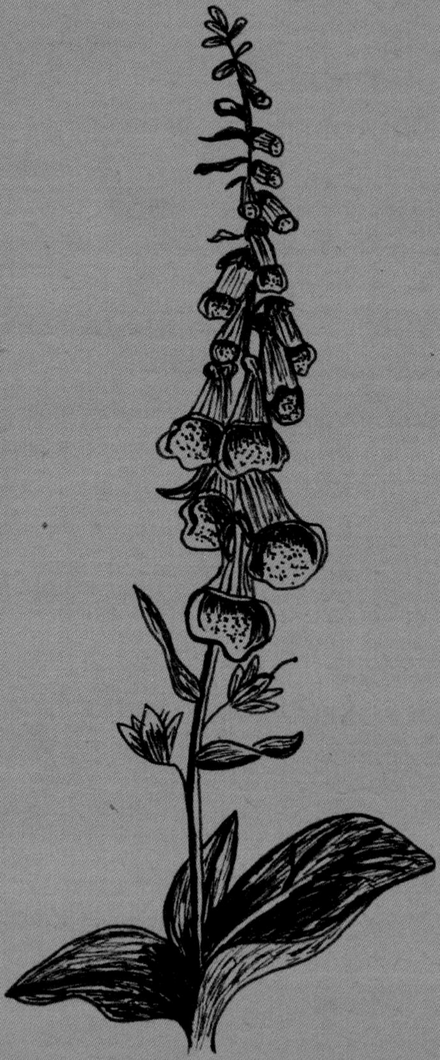

FOXGLOVE

Melt back into your
Eternal existence.

Witness the forest
Creak through time.

Watch the red sun
Dip below the tides.

Play in the sky and
Connect all the stars
In your heart.

🌹

The four of us set out on the meandering dirt path, walking the short distance from our yurt to the coastline as the sun made its way to the top of the sky. I watched as its light danced through the pine branches like a cosmic disco ball, splintering the sunshine like golden flecks of glitter. I took a deep breath of the salty wind as it blew in from the Pacific Ocean.

It was a gorgeous March day.

The magic hit as soon as our feet dipped into the warm sand, and we all became silent in the wonder. A wide smile bloomed across my face as I made my way down to the ocean and rolled up my jeans to my knees. I walked along the water's edge as the soft waves swept across my toes, and I couldn't keep my eyes off the sun's reflection in those wise ancestral waters.

That's when I sang with my feet and met the sun for the

very first time.

That white ball of energy radiated love so effortlessly, and I allowed my body to drink it in. My feet moved in time with the reverberations, and tears streamed down my face as a hint of salty seawater landed on my tongue and the wind tousled my hair. It was a beautiful dance that left me breathless as the rest of the world faded away around me. It was just me, the ocean, the wet sand, and the reflection of the sun finding a perfect rhythm together.

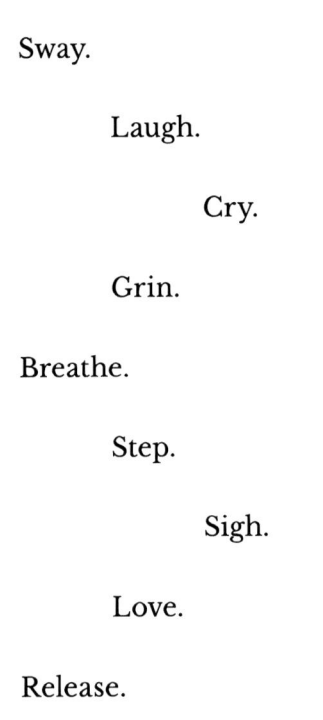

Sway.

    Laugh.

        Cry.

    Grin.

Breathe.

    Step.

        Sigh.

    Love.

Release.

When I tried to memorize that hypnotic moment so I could put it in my pocket for later, I suddenly remembered there was a whole world behind me that wasn't the ocean. I looked up and away to find the others, and there they were, right behind me, each in their own adventure.

Lia was singing with the wind.

Peter was befriending the rocks.

And Ryan, my beautiful crow man, was drawing geometric shapes in the sand with a large driftwood stick.

Yet somehow, we all moved in time together to the same beat.

I looked back at the ocean, knowing my heart and the orb were the same. The sea was just a giant mirror. I thanked it and began making my way from the water to join the others.

We hiked up to a small patch of woods just past the top of a dune where the trees were swaying and creaking. While I couldn't understand what they were trying to tell me, I knew I'd heard these sentiments before—this familiar wisdom beautifully woven into the unseen.

"What do you guys think of this spot? It's pretty flat," Lia said. We all nodded and lay down. The dirt supported our backs as we looked up at the sky and the trees for a long while, taking in their song.

When Ryan and I decided we needed to feel the sun on our faces, we left the shady woods to sit on top of the dune and look out at the ocean. All I could hear was the television static of the wind. But every time I turned around to look at Ryan's face, the world became silent, and we saw the universe in each other's eyes.

I buried my feet in the sand and let its warmth penetrate my roots. My heart was so full of pink light that my mind became utterly silent and time stood still. I felt infinity gently spiral out around me. Rivers of gilded honey making their way out to sea.

Eventually, Ryan said, "The ocean is gorgeous. I could sit here all day, but we should head back and see what Peter and Lia are up to."

"Yeah," I said, taking his outstretched hand. I shook off the warm sand from my feet, and we started trekking up the dune to join our friends.

Back in the woods, as I rested against a thick tree trunk, I saw a foxglove a few feet away in a beam of sunshine, and its magenta petals danced for me the way the flowers did when they sang *All in the Golden Afternoon* on the VHS tape of *Alice in Wonderland* I loved as a kid. I laughed, mesmerized at this reminder to embrace the kind of magic I don't usually see, but is always around me.

The day went on like this, trekking between the trees and the sand until the sun was low in the sky. And so were we.

Lia, Peter, Ryan, and I made our way back across the coastline to find the trail back home to base camp. Before we headed up the trail back to the yurt, we stopped to look back at the ocean one last time. We weren't quite ready to end this trip, so we all sat on the sand, arms around each other, and watched the red sun dip below the tides.

That's when I felt two paws on my lap. I looked down to see Wolf, partially on my lap, and partially in the sand. She looked up at me, then stuck her nose up to sniff the sultry aquatic brine in the air and closed her eyes. She was taking it all in. I closed my eyes too, and felt so much love all around me.

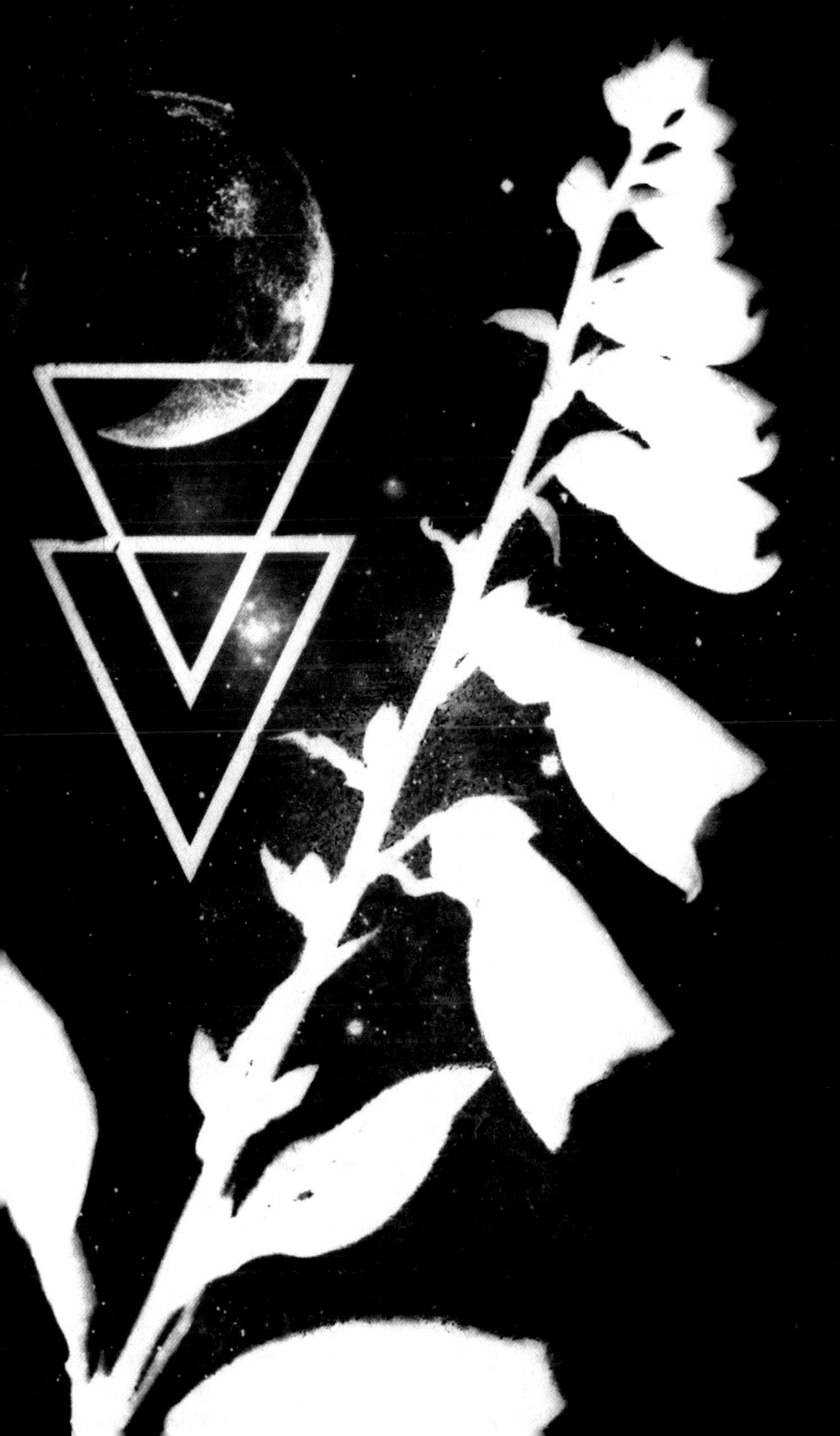

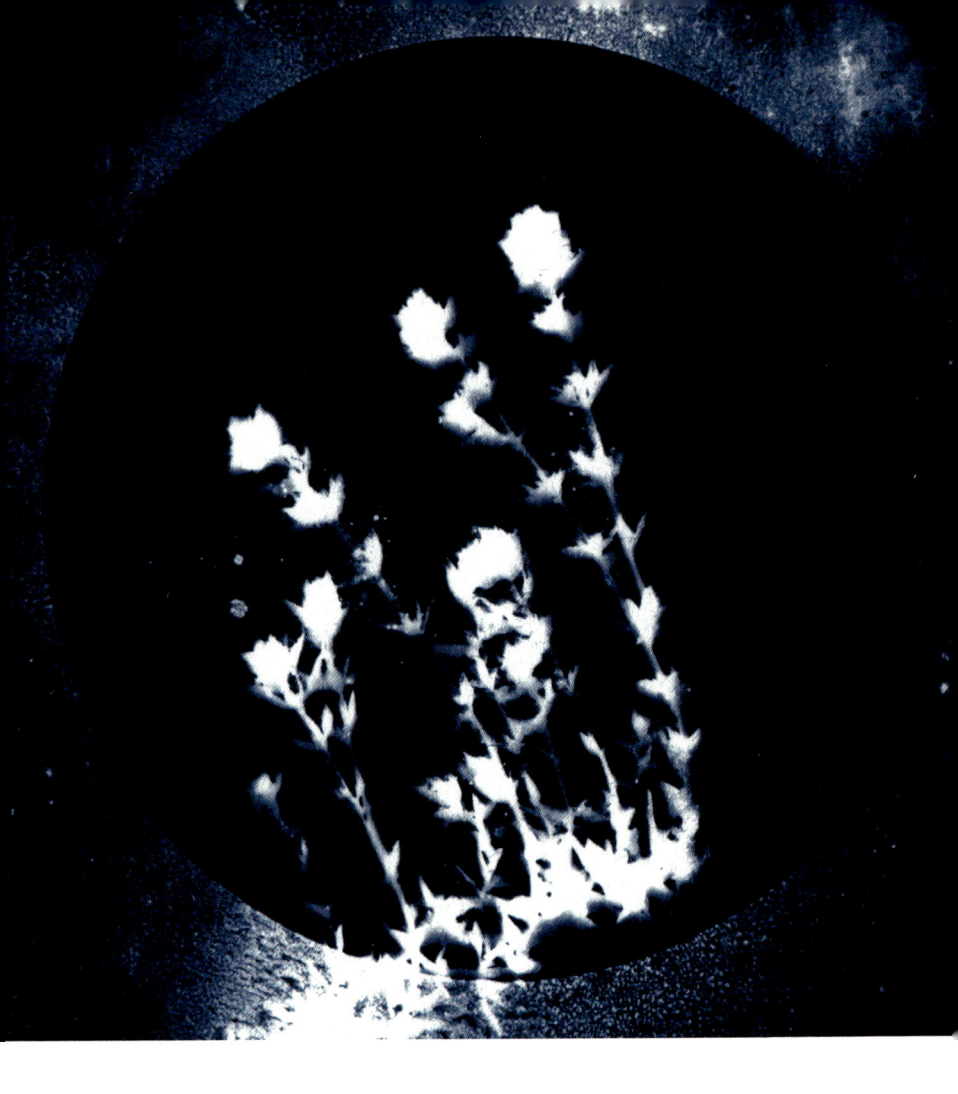

NEW HORIZONS

So hours before this New Moon, the power of Pluto, which symbolizes what is hidden and the transformation and evolution that need to happen, will be brought into collective consciousness by those photos.

—Cathy Pagano

The day the New Horizons interplanetary space probe showed the world its first photos of Pluto was the same day Mars and Mercury opposed the dwarf planet right before the new moon in Cancer.

The Secret Ceremony played a show that night at the Firkin Tavern in the heart of SE Portland, and I fell into a black hole of dread. The dark, smoky fibers followed me throughout the evening, weaving their way through my entire body until they formed a lead weight in my stomach. I got sucked in deeper as I lugged my heavy drum set from Ryan's silver Subaru Forester to the stage.

After a quick sound check, I made eye contact with my bandmates, ensuring everyone was ready, then clicked my drumsticks four times, leading us into the first song of our set. The rush of loud guitars and keyboards blasting through amplifiers created a supersonic wave, causing the lead to break apart inside my guts. Earthquakes erupted from my limbs as my performance anxiety skyrocketed through the stratosphere.
I noticed this happening more and more during our live performances, and it was getting worse.

I cleared my mind the best I could, sweeping away the urges to leave my body, and calming frantic thoughts about forgetting how to play. I wondered how my brain kept my arms and legs moving without thinking too hard? How did I keep going on autopilot through all this panic? Why were live shows becoming such an existential nightmare?

I made it through our set, and after we toted all our gear off the stage, I made my way to the bar with my one red drink ticket in my hand.

"What'll it be?" the bartender asked.

"Buffalo Trace. Light rocks. Actually, can you make it a double?"

The bartender nodded.

Over the next few days, more photos from New Horizons made their way across computer screens, and the world marveled over the complexities of Pluto and its moons. How their beauty was far beyond what anyone expected. For the first time, we witnessed its gorgeous craters, deep ravines, and ice mountains capped in methane snow stretching across its surface. Each detail sharpened in enhanced color photos, swirling together in a rich gradient of pearl, garnet, and indigo. We learned that Pluto's atmosphere is icy blue just like Earth's, and its colossal heart-shaped nitrogen glacier is the largest known in our solar system.

All of Pluto's moons are the same ancient age. NASA astrophysicists believe they formed from the upheaval caused by a single collision between Pluto and another planet in the Kuiper Belt sometime in our solar system's infancy. The week we all fawned over the dwarf planet's new glamor shots, Pluto collided with my life, and major transformations erupted at a dizzying speed.

Jasmine and Lia's rocky relationship exploded apart with a dramatic screaming match while everyone was over at our apartment for dinner. While Ryan stayed home to help Peter calm Lia down, I drove Jasmine home.

"Wasn't that so fucking funny?" Jasmine said between frenzied bouts of laughter. She had way too many beers that night.

"No, Jasmine. It wasn't." I looked her straight in the eye.

As she stumbled out of my car, she laughed again. "That was so hilarious!"

I shook my head and waved a curt goodnight before I took off down the street. I had no idea it would be the last time I'd ever see her.

Jasmine and Lia's fight lingered over the group chat for days. Ryan and I made plans to meet up with Jasmine later in the week and talk about what happened, but instead, and without warning, she left our friend group entirely by quietly blocking all our phone numbers. Her exit from our lives was unexpected and permanent. None of us have heard from her since.

The following Tuesday, I walked into band practice and told my bandmates that I loved them all, but I was quitting the band. I just didn't have it in me to play gigs anymore.

"Damn, I hate this, but I totally get it," Katy said. Dustin and Aniko agreed. We sat outside and passed around a bottle of Pinot Noir. I hugged everyone before I left.

The next morning the sun was shining brighter than usual, and the air was just starting to warm up. It was one of those glorious summer days in Portland where everyone is out and about enjoying a collective high. This is what we endured the dark, soggy winters for.

I was walking around in the courtyard behind my apartment building when I felt my phone buzz in my pocket. It was Mark's mom Teri, and since Nattie was going on a camping trip with Mark's family the following weekend, I picked it up instead of letting it go to voicemail.

"Hello?" I said as I stopped under the shade of the dogwood tree.

"Hi Christine, it's Teri." Her voice was slow, and I could tell she'd been crying.

"Hi Teri," I said, "What's up?"

"There's no easy way to say this. I'm calling to tell you Mark's dead."

At first, I didn't know who she was talking about since both Mark and his dad had the same name.

Confused, I asked, "Mark Jr.?"

"Yes," she said.

I felt a thousand pounds of metal chains lift off me. They fell to the ground with a loud, clanking thud, and I began to float a few inches off the ground.

"Shit, I'm so sorry," I said.

"Thank you. He died in his sleep last night. This is all just so shocking, and I didn't want Nattie to think her dad forgot to call her on her birthday tomorrow."

He's never called her on her birthday.

"Oh, of course," I said, "I'll let Nattie know."

"And obviously, our camping trip is canceled for now, but we plan to move it to next month and make it Mark's memorial. I hope you'll let Nattie come."

"Yes, of course," I replied, "Again, I'm so sorry, Teri. I'll talk to you soon."

I hung up the phone and caught my reflection in the glass as I walked past the neighbor's window. It had been years since I saw the black feathery wings on my back, but there they were. Outstretched and luminous, catching hues of blue and green in the glittering sun.

I flew up into the dogwood tree and peered into Nattie's room. She was sitting on the floor, cross-legged, playing her black Gibson SG guitar. Her headphones were on, and she was lost in her practice.

My breath caught in my throat.

There they were. On her back above her shoulder blades. A pair of daffodil yellow canary wings, so beautiful and strong.

It had been thirteen years, but we were finally, truly free.

Lucky 13.

ROSE

Blooming.

Sun-kissed and
Welcomed by the
Gentle breezes.

Spellbound
By the love
And beauty
Waiting to be felt.

It was there all along
Hidden in plain sight.

A RITUAL TO EMBODY LOVE AND ABUNDANCE

GATHER
- Roses - ½ to 1 cup of fresh organic rose petals (2-3 roses) or 1/4 cup dried. If using dried rose petals, pack them tight to your measuring cup, the way you would brown sugar. Red or pink roses are the most fragrant and work best for this recipe, but any roses will do.
- 1 cup filtered or distilled water
- Your smallest pot with a lid
- A small mason jar with a lid, or similar glass container. A small glass spray bottle will work best if you want to spritz your rose water on yourself or around your home.
- An open-top loose leaf tea strainer or a small piece of cheesecloth or muslin
- Timer
- Notebook or journal
- Pen or pencil
- Optional: A small piece of rose quartz

This recipe makes approximately one half cup of rose water.

Place the pot on your stove. If you have a favorite burner, set it on that one. Add in the rose petals and water. Turn the burner on and set it to medium. On my gas range, I like to put it on four.

In about two or three minutes, when the water begins simmering, cover the pot with the lid and turn the heat down to the lowest setting. Set your timer for fifteen minutes.

While your rosewater gently steeps on the stove, sit down somewhere comfortable and write two lists in your notebook or journal. The first list is ten ways you enjoy being loved. The second list is ten ways you dream of being loved.

Softness and joy are non-negotiable.

Wishing and dreaming are resistance.

Pleasure and play are radical.

Don't settle for scraps. It only goes on your list if it lights you up with excitement and makes you feel alive, appreciated, accepted, and secure.

When you hear the timer go off, turn off the stove, keep the lid on the pot, and allow your rosewater to cool completely. This usually takes around thirty minutes, but feel free to wander off for an hour or two.

Once the pot is cool to touch, wash your hands and strain your rosewater into your glass vessel using your cheesecloth, muslin, or open-top loose leaf tea strainer. Be sure to release any liquid left in the rose petals by gently pressing and squeezing them with your fingers or the back of a spoon.

Thank the roses for their magic and place them in your compost pile, if you have one. You could also bury them in your yard, garden, or in a potted plant that could use some energetic oomph.

Rosewater keeps beautifully in the refrigerator for up to a month. If you'd like, place a small piece of rose quartz on top of your jar for extra potency.

How to work with your rosewater when you need to tap into the love and abundance within and around you:

• Spritz or anoint the top of your head, over your heart, and your hands and feet.

• Add a teaspoon to any beverage. It's especially lovely in herbal teas, matcha lattes, and sparkling waters.

• Use the whole jar all at once by adding it to a warm bath with a handful of table salt and/or Epsom salts. While you're in the bath, imagine hundreds of roses pulsing at the edge of your auric field.

As you anoint, drink, or bathe in your rose water, take a few moments to tell yourself either out loud or in your mind, "I'm whole and holy in a way that can never diminish. I keep buoyant hope alive in my heart for all my desires, and know I'm worthy of kindness, softness, and love."

THE RABBIT

I pulled the car over and glanced at Ryan in the passenger seat.
He lifted the stainless steel mug from the cup holder and took a sip of lukewarm coffee.
I raised my eyebrows.
He nodded.
We both turned around and looked at Nattie in the backseat, whose wide blue eyes hoped we were about to say the words she really wanted to hear.

"Guys, we can't leave that bunny behind," Ryan said.

My heart melted a little.

He was the one who said just days before, "We're only

meeting bunnies this weekend. Let's take our time finding the right one."

"You're right. We have to go back for her," Nattie said, excitement and relief in her voice. She beamed a big smile at us, her shoulder-length bubblegum pink hair swished as she nodded her head to emphasize where she stood on the matter. Pink hair was all the rage in her eighth grade class. Looking down the hallways of Hosford Middle School was like peering into a meadow dotted with wild roses.

I put the car into reverse.

The little brown house that belonged to the folks who posted a pet rabbit on Craigslist was just a few blocks away. After we pulled back into their driveway, we all got out of the car. Ryan knocked on the front door, and when Chuck, the middle-aged dad with the silver-rim glasses opened it, Ryan said, "You know what? We'd love to take the rabbit after all."

"Ok, come back on in," Chuck said, opening the door wider for us to walk inside.

I'll never forget the tiny chihuahua who stood on the couch on high alert, barking menacingly to protect himself from the possibility of one more broken boundary. Or the tattered black cat who hissed anytime anyone looked her way. Or the cardboard box of birds in the little girl's room that I couldn't look too closely at, because I knew my heart would shatter. And I wouldn't be able to find all the broken pieces in the sea of empty food wrappers, dirty clothes, and cheap plastic toys on the stained tan carpet.

"Why are you rehoming your rabbit?" I asked the little girl. I couldn't bring myself to ask this question when we were standing here the first time. When we weren't sure we'd be bringing this rabbit home with us.

"Well, I got her for Easter, and she's not a baby anymore," she said, as she twirled her brown bobbed hair around her small fingers.

We loaded the rabbit, cage and all, into the backseat of the car. She was small and vulnerable with the softest grey and white fur and deep brown eyes. She trembled like an apple blossom bud trying to open to the late March sun, even though the bite of winter still lingered on the wind.

I promise it's gonna be ok, little bun.

We named our new bunny Murph and let her roam around the house. The walls of her cage came down, and what remained became her litter box, not her home. She eagerly munched on fresh timothy hay. And lapped up fresh water from a bowl instead of a hamster bottle for the first time in her life. We immediately threw that damn bottle away.

That first night in our house, Murph stretched her legs, and it didn't take long until she danced across our scarlet red area rug, tossing her head and twisting her little body with joy as she celebrated her newfound freedom.

Ryan, Nattie, and I basked in this fresh magic, giddy and gushing.

Still, Murph was skeptical of our intentions. At first, she wanted nothing to do with us and preferred hiding whenever we got close to her. She'd find a quick cover behind some framed pieces of art leaning up against the wall in the living room. They were artifacts of our busy lives that gave clues about our indecision over what we wanted to stare at every day.

A few weeks later, Murph began spending time under Ryan's desk, relaxing enough to flop over, exposing her soft white belly while she slept—an encouraging sign she was starting to feel safe.

Eventually, she decided she could hide out in the open, on the patches of sun streaming in through the windows, as long as she had a quick getaway.

Murph was so content to melt into the sunshine, becoming one with the puddle of light warming the hardwood floors. But as soon as I sat down next to her, she'd get spooked and hop away.

I began to wonder if she was picking up on my nervous inner landscape. I spent my whole life constructing armor around my uncertainty and fear so that most people couldn't detect it. But rabbits are sensitive, intelligent prey animals with keen intuition. Was she picking up on my shaky confidence? And was it freaking her out?

I needed to become a rabbit to find out, so I decided to shapeshift.

I began checking in with my body and emotions before approaching Murph. I'd close my eyes and take some deep breaths. Then I'd turn my eyes inward and begin searching for the physical imprints of my emotions, witnessing any grey gobs of fear tucked away in the corners of my belly, shoulders, and throat. With each breath, these emotions became unshackled, making their way out of my body, and diffusing through my skin.

Feeling a bit lighter, I'd take a few moments to breathe in pristine blue skies, allowing them to reach and illuminate every hidden corner inside me. As I did this, I found my center—a yellow glowing orb in my core that radiated calm, ancient wisdom. Once I plugged into this, I felt my energy shift from an unsteady ocean swell into clear and confident waters.

That's when Murph and I began to connect. She finally allowed me to stroke her forehead for a few moments at a time. With each hang-out session, she'd be up for a little more affection until one day, she reciprocated. She offered just a few sweet swipes of her tiny soft tongue on my hand, but I was elated, and the glowing yellow orb pulsed in unison with my tap dancing heart.

Every night we'd settle into our routine. I'd sit on the floor next to Murph and stroke her velvet face and back for thirty seconds. Then she'd lick my hand for twenty. We'd repeat this affectionate foxtrot until she'd hop away, as if to say, "Thank you. I love you. See you later."

I get it, bunny. I respect your boundaries.

I discovered Vera Stanley Alder's weird and lovely book *From the Magnificent to the Mundane* and read her stories of living in a war-torn Brittain with her sister and her pet rabbit. I fell in love with how she'd garden during the day, and travel the astral plane with one of her spirit guides at night. It was in Alder's work that I stumbled across this quote that felt as if she'd scribbled it directly across my heart:

Why is there such a special ecstasy in friendship with an animal?

As the years rambled on, Murph loved us all. She relaxed

into her spot in the family, nudging our feet for attention and head scratches. She loved to dance when she heard us rummaging in her food bag in the morning. A natural cartographer, she created a map of our house in her mind and checked her routes every morning, saying hello to all of us while she worked, clearing stray socks and lost pencils off her pathways.

She never tired of sitting in the sunshine. Or on top of the heater vent below our big picture window in the living room when the heat kicked on each winter. Every year we looked forward to getting our Christmas tree because Murph loved to sit underneath it and eat whatever tender fir branches she could reach. It was the ultimate bunny snack fort, and we were happy to provide it.

Murph's greatest joy in life, though, was eating rose petals. As soon as the hypnotic floral aroma found its way to her little wriggling nostrils, she became entranced. Alert and focused, nothing could get in the way of her favorite treat. Not the cat trying to agitate her. Not the sound of cars backfiring down Powell Boulevard. The bewitching siren song of roses would even wake her from her deepest naps. She'd thump her back paw, run out from wherever she was resting, and run circles around whoever had a rose to share.

Every May, when I spotted the first bubblegum pink rose in our backyard, I'd go out with my garden shears and clip the bloom off into my hand. The magic living inside the soft satin petals touched my skin as I walked back inside the house and waited for Murph to emerge. Our gentle hearted bunny always received this first offering of spring. This ritual infused good luck into our home and garden season after the long Portland winters. It also served as a beautiful love spell—a token of gratitude for my first familiar who taught me so much about my own energy and the beauty of learning new languages of connection.

By the time she was nine years old, Murph started showing her age. The vet told us she had arthritis in her hips, so we made sure she had plenty of soft places to rest around the house and fed her calendula flowers to help ease the inflammation. Later that same year, she suffered a stroke and stopped eating completely. That's when Ryan, Nattie, and I knew the inevitable end was upon us. We spent as much time as possible with her those last few days, making sure she was comfortable and well-loved.

I stroked her soft ears, all clear and confident waters, and whispered, "Yes, bunny. You're dying. When you're ready to let go, just follow the light."

"I'm scared," Murph said, head cocked to one side, ears alert.

I kissed the top of her head.

"I'll show you where to go," I said, tears forming in the corners of my eyes, "Just follow me."

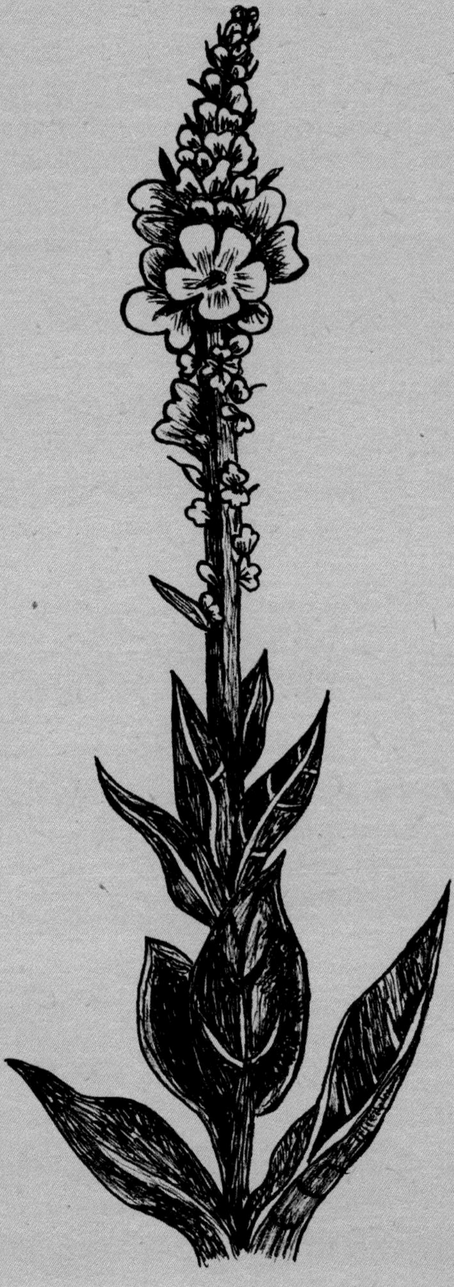

MULLEIN

Long silver streaks
Glisten softly
As she hums a
Lullaby and stirs
A pot on the flame.
"There baby," she says.
There is magic
In her strength.
And strength
In her softness.

🌿

It was a strange experience to open my eyes and find myself crouched on all fours next to Murph. I looked down at my soft, black furry paws and felt the peculiar vibrations traveling along the whiskers jutting out from my cheeks. I smelled so fresh, like pressed green hay and a hint of honeysuckle on a warm spring evening.

Murph was surprised at my transformation but still trusting. She stared at me in disbelief but didn't run away.

I twitched my nose, and gently bumped it against her shoulder, velvety smooth like a rose petal.

"We don't have a lot of time, so follow me," I said and began hopping across the scarlet red rug in the living room towards the sturdy hardwood floors of the kitchen. I kept going until we made it to a doorway near the stove and were greeted by the sage green concrete floor of the mudroom in the back of the house.

Murph had never set foot in the mudroom before,

so I leaned back on my hind legs and turned around to face her.

"We just have to go through this room, past the cat's litter box, and through the old dog door," I explained.

She nodded.

We scrambled through the mudroom towards the back door, popped through the plastic flap, and suddenly found ourselves outside. It was dusk, and rain was gently landing on the grass.

"This way," I said as I began running towards a hole in the soggy wooden fence, barely noticing the prickle of lush green grass on my fast feet. Running is its own meditation, and running as a rabbit is a different type of magic. Being so small and so close to the earth, time and space began to swirl and meld together.

Once we made it past the fence, I noticed Murph was no longer following me. Instead, she was right beside me, keeping up with my pace and finding her confidence in our mission. We frolicked and danced as we ran, twisting our delicate little bodies with gusto.

When we finally stopped under a big cottonwood tree, we were exhausted and exhilarated. The smell of rough bark and sticky sap lingered in the air between us. I looked up and recognized an old rope swing hanging down from the thickest branch. A childhood memory zipped up my spine.

We sat there for a few moments as we caught our breath. Eventually, I looked over at Murph, her big brown eyes reflecting the stars that blinked across the sky between the patchy clouds.

I sighed deeply and then paused for a moment.

"I love you so much, Murph," I said. It came out as a whisper that almost got stuck in my throat.

Murph hopped over to me so our bodies were touching, shivering together in the night air. She licked my cheek and started grooming my long satin ears, and I knew this was her ultimate show of affection. I closed my eyes and listened to the crickets chirping and the toads croaking in the distance. As I was lulled into a soft trance, a warm liquid amber filled my ribcage, and I tried to memorize how loved I felt in that moment.

The light of the full moon meandered through the branches of the old cottonwood, casting shadows on the ground below, and illuminating a large flower garden nearby. A feminine figure moved across the landscape, humming and speaking softly to the plants. She wore a pink and ivory floral top, periwinkle pleated pants, and tan patent leather slip-on shoes. Tied around her waist hung a homemade pink and purple apron with a ruffle sewn around its edge.

"You're safe here with the gardener," I said to Murph. "Her name is Mary."

Murph nodded.

I took in the details of Murph's sweet face for a few more moments. "Are you still scared?"

"No, it's peaceful here," she said. "The pain in my belly and hips is gone. I feel better than I have in days. I'm going to miss you, though. And Ryan and Nattie. But not that grumpy old cat."

I chuckled and nodded, tears welling up.

"We're going to miss you too," I whispered, "Trust me, even that weird old cat will."

Her nose twitched for a few moments as we looked into each other's eyes.

Murph turned around and hopped away, meandering through the puffy yellow dandelions and dense patches of clover, stopping to eat a blade of grass here and there. When she reached Mary, she nibbled at the hem of her periwinkle pants.

Mary looked down and said with reassuring confidence, "Well, say… hello, Miss Murph. I've been expecting you."

She knelt down and picked up Murph in the exact way Murph liked—right hand under the chest and supporting the front paws, left hand supporting the back feet and rump. Mary stood up slowly, kissed Murph on the top of her head the same way I used to, and gently placed her in the oversized front pocket of her frilly pastel apron. Before getting back to work, Mary fed Murph a handful of rose petals from the garden, then took a few moments to braid her own long, silver wavy hair, securing the end with a lavender ribbon she kept in her pocket.

I watched them for a while. Murph's head peeked out of the apron now and then to watch the spiders spinning webs between the flowers, the silky strands swinging and glowing in the moon's silver cast. Mary serenaded the towering stalks of tiny yellow mullein buds, casting her spells of love, growth and protection in the moonlight.

I heard the breeze rustling through the leaves of the

cottonwood and shivered in the chill of the nighttime air, the aromas of fresh flower petals and loamy moist soil fluttering by me. Finally, I saw Murph's little body flattening out and settling down for a snooze inside Mary's apron pocket.

A moment later, the tinkling of wind chimes from Mary's porch let me know it was time to go home. I leaned back on my hind legs, turned around, and ran as fast as I could through the night, back through the hole in the soggy fence, across the green damp grass of my backyard, and through the old dog door. As soon as my feet landed on the concrete mudroom floor, I shapeshifted back into my human form, ready for a shot of whiskey on the rocks and the longest nap I could summon.

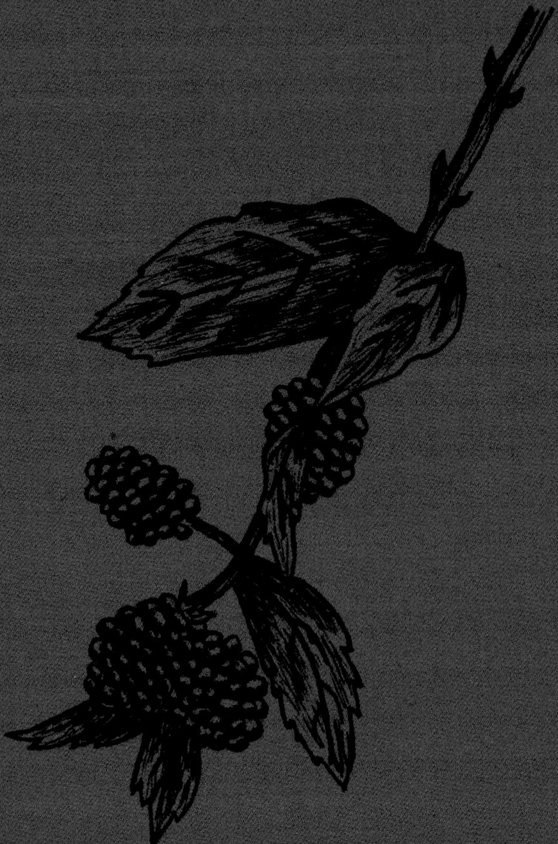

BLACKBERRY

There's a sacred trail that juts into the woods on the butte near our house.

Nattie and I like going there for long walks in the moss and trees and fresh air.

In late summer, when the sun is a high beam in the sky, the blackberries along the trail ripen into lush jewels, and our pace slows to the same meandering rhythm as the birdsong and breeze that roams through the alder leaves.

Dark juice stains our fingernails and tongues as we drink in and savor summer.

On a particularly hot August day, when the berries tasted extra sweet and the shady trail felt like a memory of autumn on my bare arms, Nattie said, "I had a dream the other night about our old apartment in downtown Camas."

"Damn, that was so long ago." I reached for a particularly plump blackberry, careful not to catch any thorns.

"Yeah. And you were there. It was that old version of you from back when you were goth, in that grungy, non-pretentious kind of way. And you still drank beer sometimes."

I flipped through the filing cabinet of my mind, to an image of myself from that era.

Twenty-two.

In a black t-shirt that hugged my curves and a black and white plaid skirt.

That mint green cardigan with the faux pearl buttons I got at Deseret thrift store on 82nd Avenue when I used to hang out with Wendy.

Black tights. Big black knee-high boots.

Long raven wings streaming down my back, and blunt Betty Paige bangs framing my young face.

My hazel eyes gazing out behind a pair of black cat-eye glasses. The ones that had the sparkling purple rhinestones in the sharp pointed corners.

"What was I doing in the dream?"

"I don't know," Nattie said, "I just remember seeing you in our old apartment and thinking, *'my mom is back.'*"

Part of me wanted to ask if she missed that old version of me, but I didn't go there. Not because I was afraid of hurting or disappointing either of us, but because it didn't matter.

I haven't been that person in fifteen years.

Instead, I just kept picking blackberries, popping them into my mouth, feeling the tartness spread over my tongue. "You know, I have dreams about that apartment sometimes, too."

"Really?"

"Yeah. It always starts the same way. I'm back in Camas,

driving down the street near the old paper mill, and suddenly I remember that I've been renting that old apartment all these years. So I go inside, and all our old stuff is still there."

That dream, although never quite the same each time, shows up every so often in the night.

Even though the rooms are painted a different color, the building is way taller than I remember, or I don't recognize my belongings, I'm always happy to know that the apartment is still mine.

Apartment number four.

I can't remember the address, but I'll never forget we lived in apartment number four. It was the first place I lived as an adult that felt like home. A one-bedroom apartment in an old brick building in downtown Camas, just a block away from the paper mill.

I adored its old hardwood floors, the rounded doorways, and the beveled glass in the kitchen nook built-ins. The dark stain of the wooden doors. The old brass door knobs with their beautiful patina. The tiny black and white octagon tiles on the bathroom and kitchen floors.

When we moved in there that mild June weekend all those years ago, I set Nattie up in the bedroom with her bed, bookshelf, and toys. Then I got to work setting up the rest of our place like a studio apartment, putting my own bed and nightstand in the corner of the living room. I hung a framed watercolor I made of a pirate woman over a hole in the wall. I was used to covering up holes in walls with posters or picture frames. These were the apartments I could afford as a young single mom.

I tried to create more of a bedroom for myself by hanging up a sheer dark purple bed canopy from the ceiling, but as soon as the smothering July heat rolled in, it became claustrophobic. I took it down, wadded it up, tossed it in the hallway closet, and convinced my parents to buy us an air conditioner that my dad installed in one of our living room windows.

I loved that apartment.

We had a little television with a VHS player. Nattie would eat microwave popcorn and watch the Power Puff Girls tape we got at a thrift store. The futon I'd had since a teenager made a fine enough couch. We splurged on a small bright pink table from IKEA to eat at. Nattie was about to turn three. That summer, I made spaghetti most nights, and she ate dinner in just her diaper and a costume pirate hat.

I had this old black cabinet that we kept all our CDs and VHS tapes in, but I adorned the top two shelves with old funeral cards of saints, statues of the Virgin Mary, and ceramic nun figurines. My divine goth altar even had a small plastic bottle of holy water I picked up at the Catholic book store near the community college I attended.

Fifteen years later, Nattie would reminisce, "*Pirates and Nuns, The Christine Blystone Story*—I mean, every goth goes through a Catholic phase." And I would smile. Not only because it was true, but because she was wise. And so accepting of her weird mom.

I'm always so surprised that she gets nostalgic about that old version of me. That young, scared, single mom who struggled so much. But to my kid, I was just her mom. I loved her a lot, and we laughed and talked and I made her spaghetti and thought it was awesome that she wanted to eat it as a wild, naked pirate.

What she didn't see was my insomnia. The nights I'd drink a lot of Goldschlager after she went to bed, in hopes that I could fall asleep that night. The nights where I'd call my friend Rob, a friend and classmate I worked with at *The Independent*—the community college's newspaper. Rob was a 28-year-old traumatized Navy veteran who also couldn't sleep. We'd talk on the phone and watch TV together. By the time *Cheaters* came on, it was nearly 3 a.m. and I had to get up in less than three hours. But I needed a distraction from the endless dark pit in my stomach that kept me awake, so we would giggle our asses off at our favorite show, and we both knew we would do it all again the next night.

I was always grateful for the nights sleep found me.

Tucked into my black sheets, under my black comforter. The tangled knot of trauma, shame, fear, and exhaustion finding somewhere else to be.

There was one night I'll never forget. I woke up around 2 a.m. to the sound of footsteps.

It sounded like someone was shuffling past my black cabinet of guardian angels. I looked over to where the sound was coming from. Even though my glasses were on the side table and my eyes were clouded with sleep, the light from the streetlamps outside meandered through my curtains and caught no silhouettes. Nobody was there.

Somehow, I just closed my eyes and went back to sleep, letting that ghost go about its business. I wasn't afraid. Even the following morning, while mulling over the late-night visit from a strange specter, I was surprised at how calm I remained.

When I was a small, round song sparrow, I started watching *Unsolved Mysteries* every Wednesday night with my dad. That show thrilled and terrified me. I became so afraid of ghosts, intergalactic beings, serial killers, and thieves that I was convinced I would be murdered, burglarized, or abducted in the middle of the night by some predator out to get me. So I slept in my parents' room for all of my childhood. I knew other kids slept soundly in their own beds, but no amount of shame could keep me from dragging my sleeping bag and pillow as quietly as I could onto my parents' bedroom floor after they fell asleep. I didn't grow out of it until I was thirteen, and even in middle school and high school I had some bad nights where I found myself making a nest on the floor with that familiar nervous pit in my stomach.

Nattie and I lived in apartment number four for two years, and when we left, I cried. We were leaving to rent a house in Portland with my boyfriend. It was right up the street from the *Portland Mercury* offices, where I had just landed a full-time job as their Web Editor. I pined for all of this for so long and somehow manifested it into reality. And I was still sad to leave the safest roost I'd ever had.

I had a revelation that summer day on the butte eating blackberries with my daughter, talking about our old life. As we kept walking down the dirt trail, I realized that Nattie was three years away from turning twenty-two. No wonder she identified so much with that old version of me.

In that moment, my heart broke open a little, and I felt compassion for my old self pour out of me. As we meandered along, the world suddenly blurred into an abstract painting of browns and greens. A tear rolled down my cheek.

"What's wrong, mom?" Nattie extended her open hand toward me.

I sighed and took the blackberry from her palm.

"Oh, I dunno. I'm just thinking about that old version of myself. How I need to love her more."

That night, I gathered my arms full of plants and blossoms I harvested with love from my garden and visited my old apartment on a night I knew I'd find myself sleeping.

I walked around in the dark and quietly blessed and protected this younger version of myself.

I brought Wolf with me, and she curled up on the foot of my old bed, her sweet head resting on my young legs.

I burned homemade incense made of cedar and lavender to clear out stagnancy.

I hung boughs of horehound and juniper above the doorways for protection.

I placed bay leaves on the windowsills to transmute fear into clarity.

I slipped passionflowers under my pillow to help me sleep peacefully.

I sprinkled hyssop in my bathtub to release shame and doubt.

And as I was placing a bouquet of yellow daffodils, purple bearded irises, and red anemones among the old ceramic nuns and statues of the Virgin Mary to amplify healing energy towards the wounds of my heart, I heard myself stir in bed behind me.

I became still and closed my eyes as I sent so much love toward my old self. Then I felt goosebumps ripple up and down my entire body.

I'm the ghost I heard shuffling around that night all those years ago.

And now I know why I wasn't afraid. It was just an older version of me, placing flowers on the altar. A caring gesture of love and protection I so desperately needed.

A RITUAL TO RECEIVE WISDOM AND GOOD LUCK

When you find yourself in a situation where you could use some clarity and good fortune, it's time to bake a blackberry crisp. While you make this dish, think about your situation, but don't toil over trying to figure anything out. Instead, just ask the blackberries whatever questions come up for you.

GATHER
- Blackberries - 4 cups fresh
- Flour - 1/2 cup (any kind will do)
- Rolled oats - 1/2 cup
- Cinnamon - 1 tsp.
- Nutmeg - 1 tsp.
- Softened butter, ghee, or vegan butter alternative - 1/3 cup
- Maple syrup - 1/4 cup (omit if you'd rather enjoy a tart dish)

Set your oven to 375 F. Grease an 8" x 8" pan. Place your blackberries in it, and thank them for the guidance you're about to receive from them.

Mix the rest of the ingredients in a bowl, then sprinkle the mixture on top of the berries.

Bake for thirty minutes, and allow to cool.

Eat your blackberry crisp over the next few days, and see what unfolds—pay extra close attention to your dreams. Journal about any epiphanies or messages you receive about your situation.

SCITO: AMA ET AUDE MILLIA*

(KNOW THIS: LOVE AND DARE (TO LOVE) A THOUSAND TIMES)

* In his book, *The Immortality Key*, Brian C. Muraresku describes an archaeological dig of Villa Vesuvio. This perfectly sealed and preserved farmhouse was buried by pumice and volcanic fragments by the Sarno River around AD 79. "Piles of organic material in the yard indicate a garden for select plants and herbs."[1] Seven vessels were found inside the house with globs of their remnants still inside. One vessel revealed a potion containing skeletal remains, including lizards, frogs, and toads, mixed with over "fifty species of plants, herbs, and trees."[2] Over half the botanicals were medicinal, including a handful that were "long associated with magic and witchcraft."[2] The biggest gem of this dig, though, was a lone piece of Latin graffiti hidden under a plaster wall inside the witch's farmhouse: *Scito: ama et aude millia*. **Know this: love and dare (to love) a thousand times.**

[1] From pg. 328 of "The Immortality Key" by Brian C. Muraresku
[2] From pg. 326 of "The Immortality Key" by Brian C. Muraresku

THE CAT

I live with a witch, and maybe that makes me a familiar.

I don't really know.

The witch I live with is powerful. She talks to plants. She ignites life over and over again, with each seed she nestles into the ground. She places her hands over the garden beds, and as light rains down from her palms and drenches the soil like invisible golden honey, she whispers, "Grow, baby, grow!"

And the seeds germinate and grow big and strong toward the sun.

And the tawny speckled deer come into the yard. They don't eat the plants—at least not the plants who are the witch's friends. Instead, the deer like to lie down, their matchstick legs gently folded underneath their soft bodies, and they bask in the magic the witch imbues into the dirt and the roots and the mycelium that all live and thrive below.

This witch also talks to me. I'm an old grey and white house cat with deep sapphire eyes and lots of mighty dark tiger stripes. I have whiskers which means I perceive a lot of things most humans can't. Like ghosts and lies and magic.

And even if you don't believe a word I just said, let me ask you this question...

Isn't there enough proof of this witch's magic in her soft thighs vibrating at a frequency that compels me—this tiny grey and white tiger—to curl up on her lap every moment I can spare? That every day I long to drape my slender furry arms over her knees, relax my chin on her earthy skin, and purr blissfully into her infinite mysteries for as long as she'll have me.

THE VORTEX

Ryan and I sat in our silver 1988 Toyota 4Runner, waiting for our first prenatal scan and doctor's appointment. We were excited and a few minutes early.

I watched from the passenger seat as a very pregnant woman walked up the sidewalk in the cold October sun.

"I'm kind of scared to have a belly that big," I admitted.

"Why?" asked Ryan.

"I can't remember if it hurts. It looks painful," I confessed.

On the darkest of days, my mind still goes back to this innocent, poignant moment.

I spent the previous nine weeks sleeping a lot and feeling nauseous even thinking about lettuce. Craving weird shit I hadn't eaten in years, like Oreo cookies. And feeling my breasts already start to swell and get tender.

We told our daughter.

We told our parents.

We told ourselves—and we let ourselves believe it.

As I sat in our truck, waiting on that beautiful autumn day, I was blissfully unaware that twenty minutes later, we'd be inside that building, shocked and sobbing, holding onto each other, as time collapsed in on itself.

In the darkness of the ultrasound room, all vulnerability and wet jelly on my abdomen, Ryan asked the tech with the long mousy brown ponytail if he could take pictures of the monitor that hung on the wall facing us.

She said, "Hold off on that."

But I still didn't suspect a thing.

Even after we left the ultrasound lab, and were led into the exam room to wait for the doctor, I said so casually, "I thought they usually let us hear the heartbeat at this appointment. I wonder why they skipped that part?"

There I sat, steeped in another innocent, poignant moment.

After the doctor came in, it was all flashes of white-hot shock.

They couldn't find a heartbeat.

I had very recently miscarried.

There was death inside me.

I felt my energy shift through a nebula into an impalpable space of darkness.

A phone call and three days later, I was back at the medical center in my socks and a shabby hospital gown, being wheeled into the operating room.

A hospital is a peculiar vortex. It's a place where some people enter this world, and it's also a place where some people exit this world. But it's even more complex and malleable than that.

The flowers know this—tucked neatly into their vases, sitting on nurse station desks and beige plastic rollaway trays—how human energy is bent in odd ways within the walls of a hospital.

People blink in and out of consciousness.

Old ghosts roam the halls.

Time collapses in on itself.

It's a liminal space.

The bright white lights and cold metal table of the operating room were such a contrast to the darkness and softness of the ultrasound lab just days before.

I felt the familiar electric shock of nerves bolt through my belly. Where will I go when I blink out of existence under anesthesia? Will I make my way back to my body?

99.

98.

97.

My eyes closed for a moment, and when I opened them back up, I found myself in the birthing center hallway, immersed in a dense fog, a nurse wheeling me back into my hospital room.

When I arrived, there was Ryan, standing in the exact same spot as when I left for surgery. His tall frame and kind, handsome face were a comfort to see. He pulled up a chair next to my bed, and I felt his hand slip into mine and give it a gentle squeeze.

I felt waves of relief wash through me as I realized I made it back to the correct moment in time and space.

No old ghosts.

Just love.

And grief.

"How's your pain?" a nurse asked me.

"About an eight," I managed to say. My voice was hoarse and my words were sluggish.

"Let's get you some pain meds."

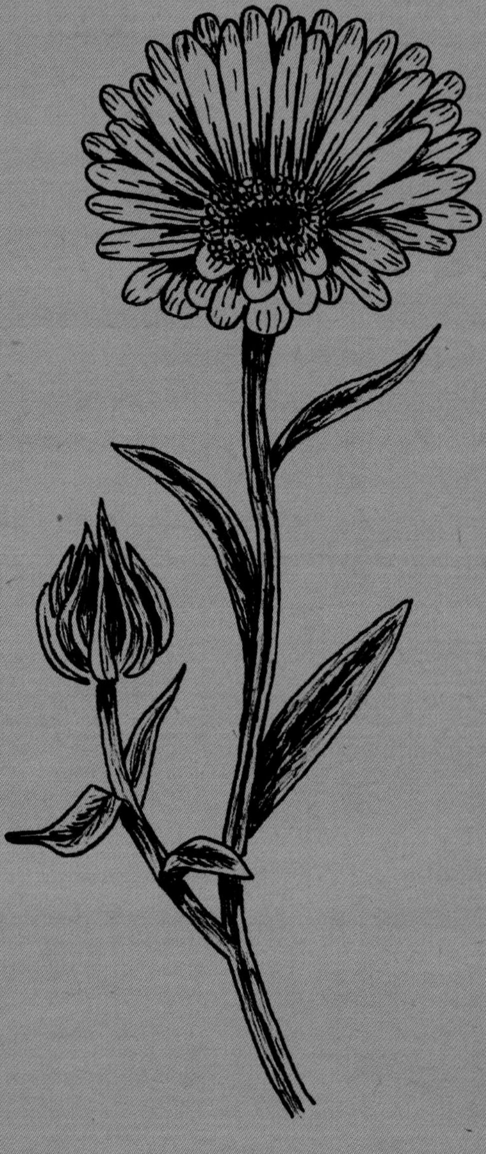

CALENDULA

A wink in the
Looking glass.

The pop of a lit
Match in the dark.

A hot cup of tea
In a wintry
Pair of hands.

An amulet carried
In the heart.

A CRONE INCANTATION

I was sitting on my back porch, heart pounding, limbs electric, tears streaming down my face.

I heaved a big breath in, then sighed it out, the last bit of air barely shaking out of me. I could see my breath curl like smoke in the shivering air, illuminated by the full moon shining down from the dark December sky.

What a shitty phone call. I felt so misunderstood. Like my grief was unworthy of empathy. Like what I was going through didn't matter.

Like I didn't matter.

That's when she stepped out from the dark corner. The old silver crone, her long hair up in milk braids, dressed in a black flowing dress, dark grey wool tights and a well-worn midnight blue velvet suit jacket. The jewelry around her neck and fingers shimmered in the moonlight.

Her face was kind and empathetic, but I could tell she also didn't fuck around. I got the sense that she was steadfast and lovely, and strong. When she looked at me, I instantly recognized her hazel eyes.

She pursed her lips for a moment, taking in an old forgotten memory. Then she clasped her hands together before speaking, all clear and confident waters.

"I know how much pain you're in," she said, taking the time to find the right words, "I know how much you need a lantern in the darkness right now. And I'm here to give you some perspective."

She crouched down in front of me, and I looked down at her feet, sturdy and strong in an old pair of weathered black leather boots that creased around the curved edges of her feet. Physical proof of all the paths she walked down throughout her life. She held out her timeworn hands. I put my own hands in hers and closed my eyes.

Suddenly, we were flying.

Two owls traversing the winter sky.

We headed north. Or maybe it was east. We flew into the soft misty clouds and tasted the cool dampness on our tongues. We heard the wind howl around us as we silently glided through time.

At daybreak, we found ourselves surrounded by tall green ridges covered with majestic trees. We spotted an old cabin below us and landed on the peak of the black tin roof. The sweet smell of burning oak logs wafted from the brick chimney, and it swirled around with the fresh scent of the surrounding firs. I took in a big cleansing breath, filling my whole belly.

I looked around and saw a home created with love and care. There were gardens of food, flowers, and herbs. A wood-fired cedar hot tub for healing and resting. A big barn I just knew housed so many tools and projects and bicycles. I spied the silhouette of a vintage red and black Pearl drum set through the open doorway. Further out, I could barely make out a little brick building with a sign on the door that read: *Fuck off. I'm writing.*

The silver owl descended from the roof and flew down to the front porch, landing on the ledge of a big window. I followed her, and we peeked inside the house.

I still couldn't see who lived here, but their stories were imprinted everywhere.

A pot of sweet-smelling chamomile and ginger tea sat on the kitchen table.

An old black cat slept peacefully, stretched out on the comfy worn-in sofa.

Bundles of bright orange calendula and fragrant lavender hung from the wooden rafters.

Books of every color and thickness were tucked in all the nooks and crannies, their thumbed pages perfumed by aging ink and paper.

An old turntable set up in the corner spun *Gimme All Your Love* by the Alabama Shakes, those big, slow drums gently stepping closer towards me with every beat while the melodic organ notes rang out like a singing bowl. I could hear it all through the glass as Brittany Howard serenaded me with, "So much is going on, but you can always come around…"

A lifetime of art-making hung from the walls. And so many photos of faces with joyful eyes.

Chubby-cheeked babies in soft pastel pajamas showing off their drooly toothy grins while sitting on homemade quilts.

Dirt-smeared kids on bicycles.

Wild-haired teens playing guitars, trying to look cool as they tried on different personas.

Old friends gathered around a campfire, clutching cans of ice-cold beer plucked straight from the cooler. Some of them passed around a bottle of whiskey.

Generations gathered around a table of fried fish, coleslaw, and homemade German chocolate cake, celebrating a beloved grandmother's ninety-third birthday.

Important milestones.

Relics of family journeys to new places.

And those heartbreakingly small moments that you don't even realize how much they matter until you find them later, printed on glossy paper, tucked away in a forgotten envelope or box.

One look instantly tugs at your heart, so you time travel them back to the present moment with a loud thwack of a magnet on the refrigerator door.

I recognized so many of these faces and memories and suddenly realized what I was witnessing.

I looked over at the silver owl, but she was gone.

I heard a soft laugh behind me and turned around.

The old silver crone, her long hair up in milk braids, dressed in a black flowing dress and her enchanted talismans, grinned at me from her rocking chair on the porch.

"See? It'll all work out," she said gently, with a quick wink and a soft, friendly grin.

She paused for a moment, putting her right hand over her heart, so much love in her eyes.

"Please don't forget how much you matter to those who show up and go deep with you.

Anyone who doesn't take the time to understand you and what you're going through, who can't be tender with your heart, or who gets offended by your boundaries because they refuse to be curious about your pain and what they can do to help you heal—well, don't allow their bullshit to dim your magic. Not for one second.

You are love. And you are worthy of love. Always."

A RITUAL TO CALL IN UNWAVERING SUPPORT AND BADASSERY

Rushing through the fields and flowers
Her voice coming through my dial
She's the one, I swear to God
A frequency, she's got a frequency
And I want it all over me

— Sylvan Esso

Part of my healing practice involves sending love and support to younger versions of myself that didn't get their needs met at the time. I started doing this with the help of my therapist, and the more I practiced, the easier it was to access throughout my daily life. As I journeyed deeper into this magic, I had a moment of sudden insight where my current self sensed an older version of me sending love and blessings from the future.

When you find yourself in a season of your life when you need to lean on unwavering support and badassery, create a loving altar to call in your ancestor self.

In addition to the items below, you'll also need to pick a flat place to build your altar. It can be as big or as small as you'd like.

Some of my favorite places to build altars are:
• On top of a dresser
• On a shelf—either the whole shelf or whatever portion you can spare
• On a windowsill

- Under a tree in the yard
- A special spot in the garden
- The inside of a cupboard door works really well if you'd like to build an altar out of flat paper ephemera

GATHER
- Notebook or journal
- Pen or pencil
- A hot cup of your favorite tea

Find a comfortable place to sit and write for the next ten minutes or so. Make sure you take the time you need to be comfortable before you begin.

When you're ready, close your eyes and take a deep breath, inhaling slowly and deeply into your belly. Hold your breath there for a few moments, then release. Go ahead and take two more deep breaths like this, and allow your breath to soften any areas in your body that might be tight or holding onto something from your day.

Now spend the next few minutes imagining your ancestor self. What do they look like? What are they wearing? Where do they live? How do they like to spend their time? What characteristics stick out to you? Encourage your mind's eye to bring in as many precise details as possible, then jot down any impressions you get in your journal.

Set down your journal, and switch your focus to your cup of tea. Take a few sips and allow your body to relax a little further. Keep sipping your tea until you're ready to move on to the next step of this ritual. This break in the middle will help you look at what you just wrote with fresh eyes.

Explore the list you created in your journal, and think about how you'd like to honor your ancestor self through an altar. If you get stuck or overwhelmed, remember this: Your ancestor self is you. Chances are, many things that would honor them would also honor your current self. Make a list of these objects in your journal. They don't need to be fancy, and you absolutely don't need to buy anything.

Some of my favorite things to include in altars:
- Photographs
- Images cut out from magazines
- Words inscribed on small scraps of paper
- Hand-written letters and poems
- Drawings, collages, and paintings
- Tarot and oracle cards
- Postcards and other ephemera
- Cut flowers and plant clippings (fresh or dried)
- Seedpods and pinecones found outside on the ground
- Spices from your cupboard
- Rocks, gems, stones, and shells
- Small trinkets and statues

Once you've gathered your meaningful objects, intuitively arrange them in a pleasing shape on your chosen altar space. Take your time and move things around until you find an arrangement that feels like a hell yes in your core.

Whenever you sense your future self rooting for you and sending nurturing emotional care packages from the other side of time and space, say a simple, "Thank you," either out loud or in your mind. Make a note to tidy up and refresh your altar in any way that feels right to you.

RHODODENDRON

Confide in
A soft sigh
So familiar
It makes a
Delicate nest
In your hair.

Build a long
Wooden table
To fill with
Nourishing
Laughter.

Dig in the dirt
And root into a
Strong foundation
Of growth and
Commitment.

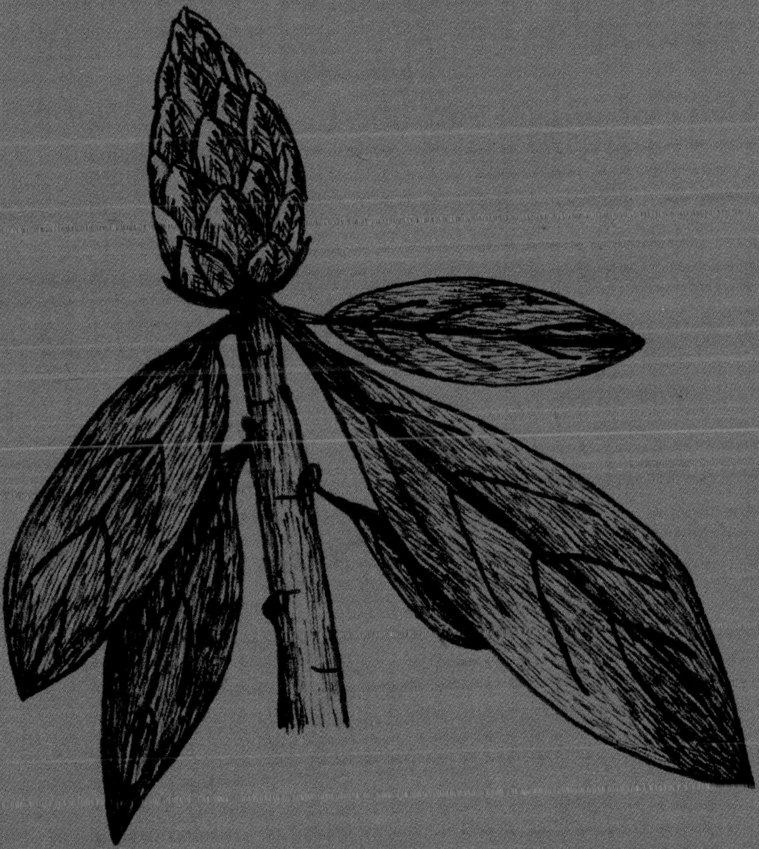

THE SILVER BULLET

The day Ryan brought home a shiny aluminum 1998 Cannondale tandem mountain bike, I took one look at her and said, "She looks like a can of Coors Light."

We both laughed, our eyes framed by the crow's feet of a hard year where all our plans just didn't work out.

It was in that moment we christened our new ride the Silver Bullet.

I know a lot of people who describe cycling as pure freedom, but that's not me. I turn into a scared prey animal whenever I get on a bike. For the first fifteen minutes, I'm all shaking limbs, wide eyes, and an acrid feeling in my stomach. After I get used to pedaling, I can relax a little bit into the experience, as long as I'm not sharing the road with cars or too many hot shit cyclists who zoom around me.

In general, I prefer less crowded spaces and more room to roam.

And I almost always favor my own two sturdy legs to any other form of getting around.

So when I got on the back of the Silver Bullet, and Ryan explained all I had to do was put my feet on the pedals and hold on to the handlebars, I couldn't quite trust something new. My feet were on the pedals, sure, but my right hand clutched the chain-link fence along our driveway.

I couldn't let go.

I've never been very good at leaps of faith, and the way the past year still clung to my body wasn't helping me feel optimistic.

The year started with two dear friends moving 2,492 miles away. There were promises of staying close, but I'm no stranger to the strain and heartache of long-distance relationships. There's an intimacy that's lost when animal bodies used to sharing Sunday dinners and late-night talks around a campfire suddenly become invisible, intermittent voices on the other end of the line.

The Oregon wildfires burned up so much of the state, and Portland had the most toxic air in the whole world for the entire end of summer. We stuffed blankets under the doorways and simmered rosemary, thyme, and sage on the stove. This kitchen potion was an energetic prayer for protection, and it also helped cut the thick, choking smell of our beloved forests endlessly incinerating around us.

It was also the year Murph suddenly got sick and passed away.

And then I had the miscarriage.

And the frustrating, painful health issues that came afterward.

Even though it had been almost eight months, I still wasn't ovulating. My periods were long and heavy. It took me nineteen years to be ready to have another baby, and now my womb was stuck in an echo chamber of grief, unwilling to move on.

I took a deep breath, let go of the fence, brought my trembling hand to the handlebar, squeezed my eyes shut, and said, "Ok, go!"

Thankfully Ryan kicked off on the Silver Bullet before I could change my mind.

The wobbly start immediately shapeshifted me into my rabbit form. My black fur trembling, heart racing under my breastbone, all muscles tense, eyes darting, looking for an escape. We rode around our neighborhood, worked out our rhythm for pedaling, and figured out how to start and stop this new conjoined extension of our bodies.

Ryan turned his head so I could hear him, "You ready for the Springwater Trail?"

"Fuck it, let's go," I said.

The Silver Bullet is a smooth ride.

The weight of the bike and our bodies on the pavement allowed my nervous system to relax a little. I immediately loved that I didn't have to mess around with gears or navigate traffic. That was all Ryan. All I had to do was pedal and be the sturdy engine.

I'm good at that.

"You wanna go down that big hill to get onto the trail?" Ryan yelled into the tailwind.

"Yeah, I trust you!" I said.

So down we went. We turned the corner onto the trail a lot faster than I would have ever gone on my own. I felt nervous about it at first, but when I realized how easy it felt to zip around that little intersection, I memorized how that felt in my body.

The Silver Bullet is a swift ride.

We flew up hills like we were gliding on wings. I began to see cycling through Ryan's eyes, as he easily navigated around other folks on bikes and families walking along the trail. His confidence was contagious. I loosened my tight grip on the handlebars and adjusted my position on the saddle.

I began to feel my umber owl feathers return, shaking off the dust.

When we reached the end of the Springwater Trail in a little town called Boring, we hopped off the bike and caught our breath at the stoplight, exhilarated at how much fun we were having as our bodies synced up even more. We were getting the hang of this.

And it was starting to feel like freedom.

I turned my head to face Ryan. "I love this fucking bike!"

Ryan's kind blue eyes sparkled, as a big smile stretched across his face. "Yeah? I can't wait to show you this next trail."

We took the Silver Bullet across the street on foot, then got back on her and descended down a long hill. When we reached the bottom, where the air felt cooler on our faces, the path turned to gravel. Lined with old-growth trees and a beautiful creek flowing along one side, our cadence slowed down to meet the rhythm of the wilderness.

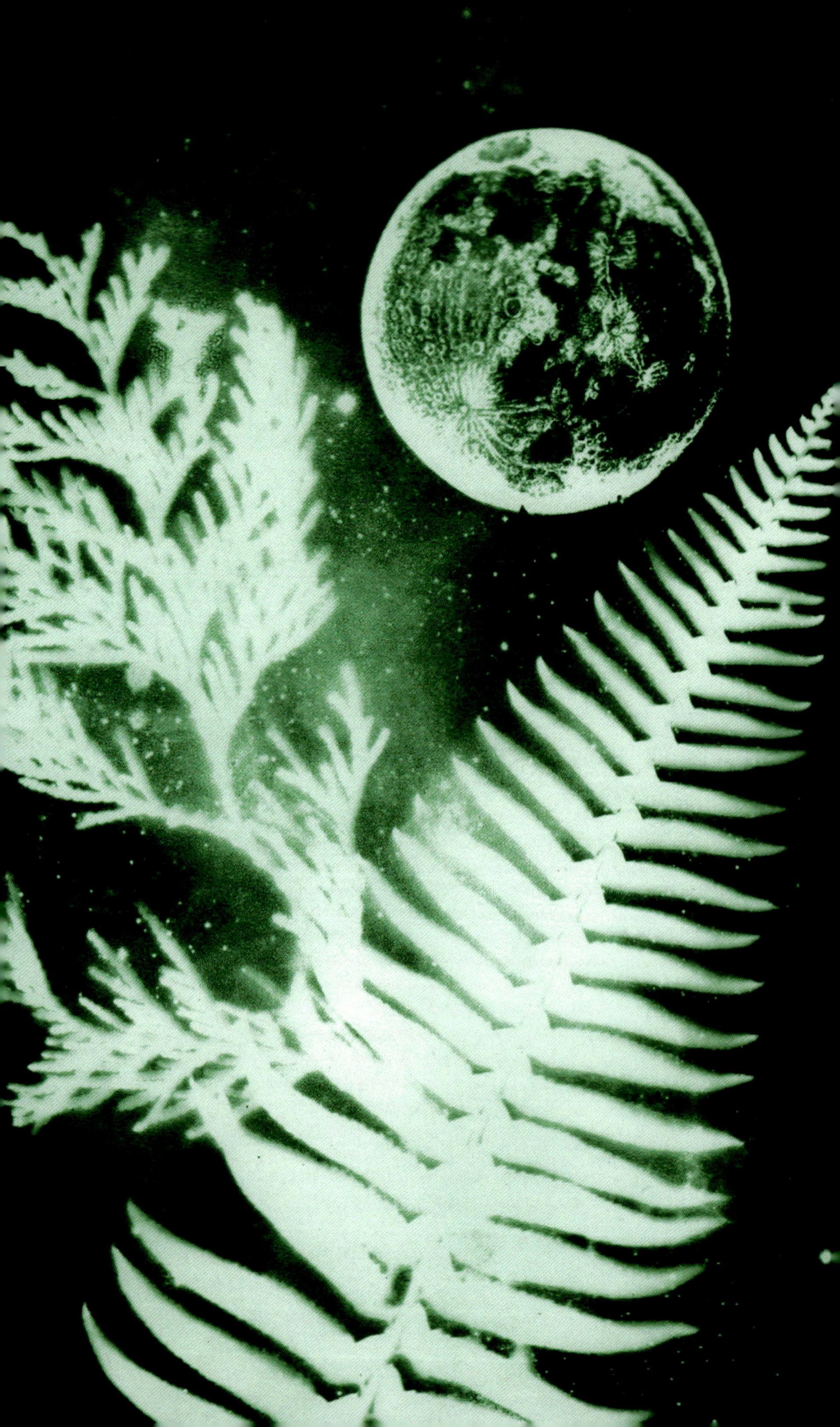

Soon we could smell moss and dirt warming in the sun, and the breeze brought with it the whisperings between the blackberry leaves, still spring-tender and almost translucent, and the towering green nettles.

I savored this moment, fully letting go and trusting in the journey. Finally.

I felt so alive and connected to something bigger than myself.

That's what relationships are supposed to feel like, right? I knew Ryan would never do anything that could harm me. Not like past lovers. Not like they did. Ryan wouldn't let me fall off this bike, or try to make me feel small or degraded.

The previous season beat us up pretty bad, and even though our hearts were still bruised and tender, here we were, leaning into each other's strengths so we could be better together. Holding onto each other and helping each other find joy.

After we passed through a grove of huge flowering rhododendrons, I looked down at our synchronized feet, the trail beneath us a blur.

Suddenly, I was reminded of a time when Ryan was a city crow living in New York, and we met in this forest, both perched in a tall douglas fir.

I placed my hand gently on Ryan's back. The same hand that was terrified to let go of the fence in our driveway just an hour before.

"Have I told you how much I love this fucking bike?"

THE BAT

When I wasn't quite so young anymore, and my hair was a nest of dark brown and silver owl feathers, I found a hidden cavern deep inside my rib cage. It was so wide, it spanned across my heart and up into the backs of my shoulders.

A deep black pool of water lived in the middle of this tall grotto. I didn't even need to touch the shiny surface to feel how heavy it was. Simply standing on the dusty, grey rocky edge made the back of my nose sting. Tears formed in the corners of my eyes as the weight of its contents wrapped around my bones.

I'd spent my whole life living in a culture that taught me I wasn't worthy of love if I had any emotional needs at all. Putting up boundaries to keep myself safe was unacceptable, especially if it made anyone else uncomfortable. And feeling any human emotions the world deemed ugly resulted in endless shame.

Anger. Hurt. Fear. Sadness. Lust. Envy. Rage. Into the pool they all went, disowned and aching.

Sometimes I'd work with the pull of the full moon to empty out these murky waters, feeling the waves of all those lost emotions and allowing them to flow down through my belly, passing through my left thigh, until they eventually released out from the bottom of my foot.

This made me feel lighter and full of hope.

But when the second miscarriage happened, the harsh waters came crashing back in, and refilled this well of sadness with all of the old pain I'd worked so hard to let go of. A lifetime of intense sorrow and rejection swirled in the deep watery abyss, telling the same old stories that zapped the magic right out of my blood.

Other people get to live their dreams. Not you.

Frustrated and exhausted, I tried to deny this dark pool's existence. Every time it tugged at my sleeve, I yelled out profanities that reverberated around the grotto until they echoed endlessly inside my mind.

Not this bullshit again.

Fuck, I'm so tired of feeling this way.

God damnit, when does it get any easier?

The incessant grief took over my body, and made it nearly impossible to feel the the yellow glowing orb in my core that radiated calm, ancient wisdom.

One night while I was sleeping, the orb traveled up along my spine, and visited me in a dream. Sensing my desperation, it gently whispered to me, "The truth is that your dark waters need a safe place to be accepted, no matter how much it feels like the weight of it all will crush you."

Six weeks after the second miscarriage, Ryan and I were getting out of our car in the driveway, when our neighbors who have a one-year old daughter saw us and made their way around the huge western redcedar that separates our front yards.

"We're pregnant again—expecting in May! We just had our first ultrasound today."

The brisk early autumn air stopped moving. I felt that familiar sinking feeling in my stomach, and the lightheadedness that comes with a difficult surprise. I smiled and congratulated them, then found a moment to excuse myself and walked toward my front door. I took my keys out of my bag and my heavy hands fumbled with the lock. I couldn't get inside fast enough. The well of sadness overflowed from my chest, and spilled out all around me. Dark waters emanated from my eyes. It had nowhere else to go.

The next day Ryan and I were on a video call with our friends who moved 2,492 miles away, and we saw their three-month-old baby girl for the first time. That was also really hard.

"How are you?" Ryan asked me, after he hit the big red button on his phone screen, ending the call.

"Eh, I'm ok. Still processing. How are you?" I asked.

He stood up and lingered in the entryway to the living room. "Sad. That was so much harder than I thought it was going to be."

Nobody really understood why those cooing baby sounds hit our bodies like piercing arrows, because everyone is taught that babies are supposed to make everyone happy. Even folks grieving two lost pregnancies.

It's not that we weren't happy for our friends, our neighbors, or any other pregnant belly we encountered—we were. It's just that we had other feelings too. Feelings that had nothing to do with them or their happiness, and everything to do with the grief and trauma of our own losses. Still, they seemed to take those feelings personally.

Maybe they were simply terrified. I understand why expectant parents can't stand to look too closely at what Ryan and I have been through. It would mean taking a peek behind the thin veil that separates life and death and truly understanding how fragile life is. I'm sure it's scary as hell to feel that fear in their guts and bones, and to realize the futures we dream of are even more fragile than the tiny seedling they're incubating and preparing to bring into the world.

Still, why did it always feel like we were expected to meet others in their joy without anyone meeting us in our grief? All I wanted was to meet in the middle with some boundaries so everyone could feel supported and get their needs met. And so I could heal. I was exhausted, hurt and angry from the expectation that I should abandon myself over and over again so that everyone else felt comfortable.

Eight weeks after the second miscarriage, Ryan and I decided it was time to hit the road. It was late in October, so we loaded up our old silver Toyota 4Runner with two old Coleman sleeping bags, enough sandwich fixings for a week, and a few duffel bags full of our warmest clothes, and we headed toward southeastern Oregon.

Our first stop was a campground called the Priest Hole, nestled along the John Day River. We arrived a few hours before dusk and parked on the dry river rock bed right along the water. Tall brown rocky hills surrounded us. When I stepped out of the truck, something sweet and pungent that reminded me of tiny sunshine-yellow immortelle flowers drifted softly in the air.

It was quiet, too. All we could hear was the soft song of the river flowing by.

At twilight, I wandered off by myself and a little black bat found me, circling high above my head. I watched her beautiful crepe paper wings flutter like an old stop-motion animation. Her tiny body seemed so at home in the sky.

"Follow me—I have something to show you," she squeaked.

She wasn't the only bat of the season. The first one came to me in a dream in early September. Her bony brown feet landed on my left hand, and I was terrified she would bite me at first. I relaxed when I sensed she was a friendly guide just delivering a message, but I woke up before she could impart her wisdom. A few weeks after that, I was thumbing through a fall seed catalog and found an illustration of a bat flying above a field at sundown. I cut it out and put it on my altar.

Ok, I'll follow you, little bat. You've been trying to send me a message for a while now.

The next morning, as Ryan and I finished our hot mugs of green tea, we watched a silent herd of deer cross the robust currents to the furthest riverbank from where we sat. They gently walked into the river, their soft and speckled tan bodies lowering further and further below the surface with each step until just their ears and black noses danced on the top of the water. Once the last deer made safe passage to the other side, the little group continued on their way, heading toward a secluded patch of tall grasses to relax and graze in. Ryan looked at me and said, "Damn, that was so cool. Ready to pack up and get the day started?"

I nodded.

I wasn't sure if Ryan could see the little black bat or not, but we followed her to the Painted Hills, which formed thirty-five million years ago when the area was an ancient river floodplain. The rocks and minerals that make up the rounded peaks continually morph in tone and color, depending on the light and weather—which meant we'd never see the hills the same way we did that day.

We walked up a short rocky trail to the viewpoint and stared at the intense bands of spring green volcanic ash, rust red iron oxide, and basalt black manganese mounded up towards the sky. They were breathtaking.

"It reminds me of something from a Dr. Suess book," I said.

"Yeah, like we just stepped into the cover of *Oh the Places You'll Go*."

We took it in for a while, listening to the wind whip around our heads, until the bat flew by and we walked back down the rocky path, hopped back into the truck, and continued on through the endless fields of sagebrush desert. We spotted mule deer and black and white magpies along our journey through the John Day Fossil Beds, heading toward the Steens Mountains.

"Holy shit!" I said, as a gorgeous great blue heron took flight right in front of us on Highway 20, just north of a small town called Burns.

Ryan slowed down so we wouldn't hit it. As its long, slender, massive body flew past our windshield, images of pterodactyls danced in my mind.

Ryan smiled. "Man, I love where we live."

A few hours later, we found ourselves driving through the lodgepole pine forests, making our ascent into our final destination for the night. We stared in awe at the enormous larches, with their needles ablaze in golden yellow hues. We made it to the South Steens Mountains Campground after dark, and were so worn out from a full day of driving that we quickly ate our chicken sandwich dinners and tucked ourselves into our sleeping bags in the back of the truck.

That night the little black bat visited me while I slept.

I found myself in a long dark hallway full of closed wooden doors, each stained a dark walnut hue with its own beautiful old brass doorknob. Some of the knobs were oval and slender. Some had intricate key holes. Others were fat and round, stamped with engravings of mugwort, spiders, moonflowers, and ferns. The black and white checkerboard floor seemed to stretch on forever, becoming a tiny speck in the distance. My shaking hand held onto a dimly lit torch. I wandered the hallway, searching for clues. I had no idea where I needed to go.

"Your heart knows the way," the bat said as she swooped above my head, "You've got it from here. The next time you see me, you'll understand what I came to show you."

I saw a door up ahead with an antique purple glass doorknob. It seemed to be illuminated by a skylight in the ceiling. I sped up my pace, hearing my black leather boots squeak against the tile floor, the smell of burning wood and smoke from the torch trailing behind me. I grabbed the doorknob and gave the heavy door a huge push with the entire weight of my body.

I woke up to sunlight and the crisp air that comes with

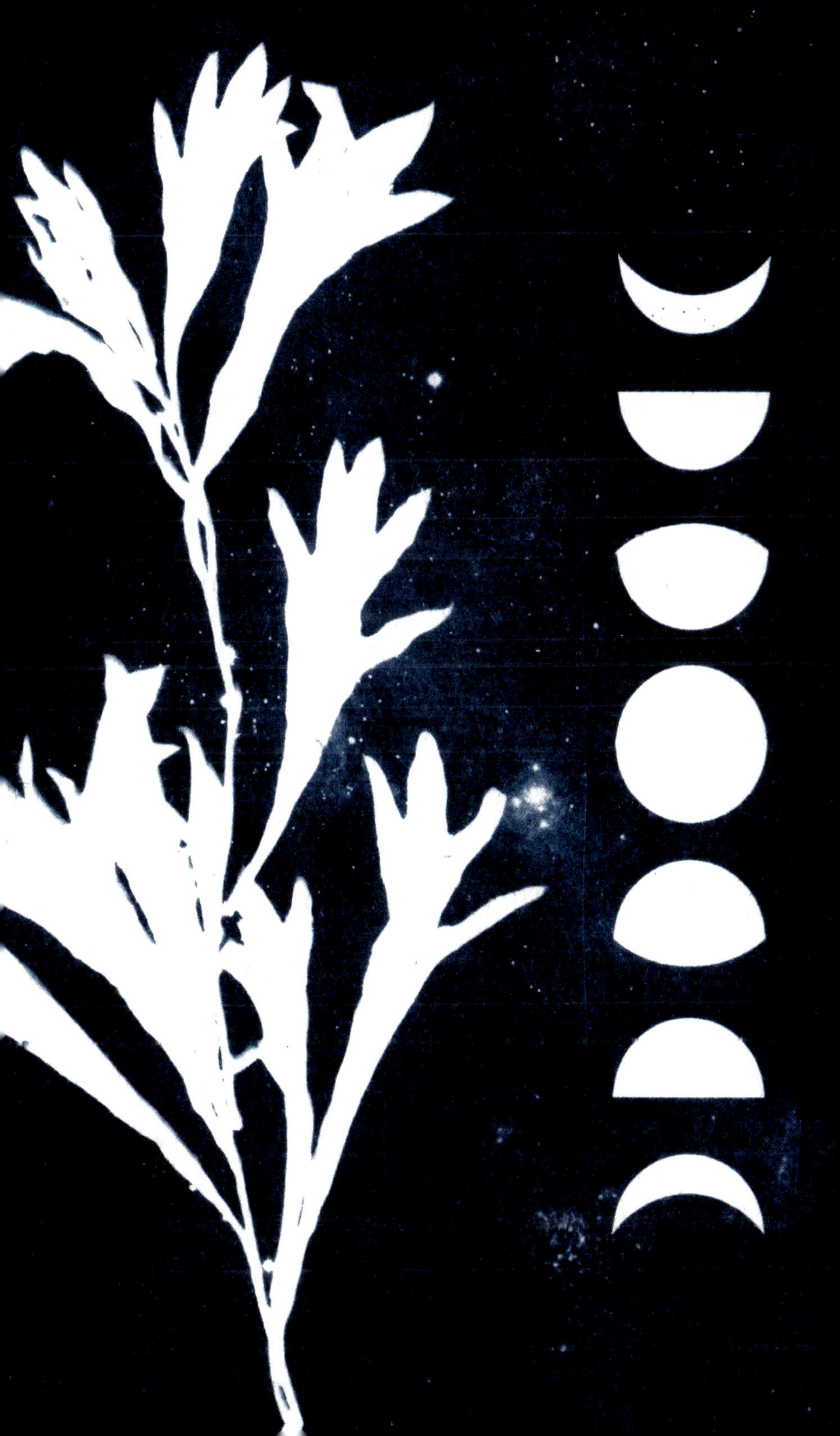

fresh rain. I stumbled out of the truck and took a deep breath in and let the fragrant aroma of camphor drifting off the sagebrush cleanse me. Before we got back on the road, we filled our water bottles with the cold mountain water from the campground's wellhouse, then took off to find the Alvord Desert.

It was twenty miles to the main road, and by the time we stopped to watch the wild mustangs grazing in the morning sun, with just the sound of the wind in my ears, I felt different inside my body. My mind felt quiet, and my shoulders soft. Ryan and I had finally shed life's electric trappings, and that relief washed over our bodies, creating a soothing silver stillness that stretched out all around us. At last, I could tune into the frequency that picked up information the way my animal body was built to receive it.

Ryan watched the horses through our binoculars. His hair cascaded down his neck and formed soft waves at the tops of his shoulders. They glistened like honey in the sunshine.

Ryan looked over at me and held out the binoculars. I took them and watched the caramel colored horses up close for a while, in awe of their wild strength and the palpable softness between them.

I tucked the binoculars back into their case. "Ready to hop back in the truck and keep going?"

Ryan nodded, "Yeah, I can't wait to get to the Alvord. I've wanted to see it for years."

An otherworldly place, the Alvord Desert is a dry lake bed in the rain shadow of the Steens Mountains where the earth is thick and broken like old ceramic tiles. We arrived in the early afternoon, just as the half moon was setting below the Steens.

We drove the truck out to the middle of the playa and enjoyed a spectacular sunset that danced across the fluffy clouds, dressing them up in vivid orange silks and rich magenta taffetas. Once nightfall arrived, the temperature dropped quickly, so we climbed into the back of the truck where we were safe from the biting wind.

Ryan woke me up in the middle of the night to gaze at the moon. It hung low and huge on the horizon, fertile and gilded in its glow.

"Wow, look at that moon," I breathed, gazing out the back window of the truck.

"You're the moon," Ryan whispered in my ear, and spooned me close as we drifted back to sleep.

When the sun rose the next morning, slowly transforming the dark skies into lighter and lighter shades of blue, we packed up our truck and headed west toward Hart Mountain Hot Springs. We spotted wild bighorn sheep on the way there, munching on the neverending fields of shimmering tan grasses. We didn't stop to watch them, but a few hours later, when we found ourselves on a bumpy gravel road in a vast stretch of flat plains, we pulled over to watch a herd of north american pronghorn for a while.

"Check them out," Ryan said softly, handing me the binoculars, "These guys are super old creatures. They're the only surviving member of a group of animals that were here twenty million years ago."

I peered at the ancient creatures through my spyglass.

They're more closely related to giraffes than deer, giving them an almost supernatural radiance.

"I wonder what wisdom they hold in their bodies from their Pleistocene ancestors?" I asked quietly, careful not to let my voice travel on the wind.

Ryan looked back at me, a big grin on his face. He loved to think about this kind of stuff.

We made it to Hart Mountain in the golden incandescence of the afternoon and found a campsite nestled into a valley near a cove of willows on a slow-moving creek. It was just a quick walk to the hot spring.

Ryan and I waited until it was dark to take a dip, and we got lucky that night with a clear, bright sky full of stars. We walked up the dirt path to the hot spring, dressed in just our bathing suits and puffy down coats, while the bitter autumn wind whipped around our bare legs. The light of the moon led the way while we shivered and stepped quickly through the night.

When we approached the water, I froze.

Astonishment washed throughout my entire body, starting as a prickly wave at the top of my head, then undulating down to the tips of my toes and back up again.

There it was. That deep black pool of water. The same one I found in my ribcage. I had no idea how deep it was. I couldn't see the bottom, just the moonlight shimmering on its dark surface and the wet stone ledges around it. A crust of white minerals along the waterline glowed in the dark.

I'd sat here so many times, yet this time was different. This time I wasn't alone.

And I was going in.

I stripped off my coat and headed for the little metal ladder at the edge. I grabbed each side and crouched on the top rung. Hot water washed over my feet. I exhaled. I extended my right leg down a few rungs. Then my left leg. Hot water hugged my waist.

"How does it feel?" Ryan asked from the shore.

"Amazing," I said, "Get in here!"

My feet found the uneven rocks along the bottom of the pool while my hands grasped all the algae around the exposed rim. The smell of minerals and damp stones became more potent with each step. I turned around and spotted a rock formation jutting out from one side of the spring, so I made my way over and sat on it, just my neck and head above the water in the chilly night, the rest of my body submerged in warmth below.

"There's room for one more butt over here," I said, and Ryan sat next to me in the soft, comfortable waters of the earth's womb. We put our arms around each other and held each other tight, and felt the earth hold us in return.

We sat quietly for a moment, allowing the steamy air to warm our faces. I could hear Ryan's wet hair dripping onto his shoulders, and as the silky hot water kept sliding over our skin, I felt our bodies releasing more tension as our aches and pains faded into oblivion.

We kept looking up at the giant dome of stars above our heads as bubbles rose from the bottom of the pool.

"How far down do you think those bubbles are coming from?" Ryan wondered.

"I'm not sure, but wouldn't it be cool if it was so much further down than either of us could ever guess?"

All I knew was that each bubble was the earth whispering her blessings to us.

You are safe.

You are loved.

You are worthy of your dreams.

That's when I saw the little black bat fly overhead, past the arm of the milky way galaxy, as a shooting star streaked across the sky.

"Wow! Did you see that one?" Ryan asked.

"I sure did," I said, squeezing his hand underneath the wild dark womb waters. I kissed his cheek and tasted the ancient mineral brine of creation in his beard.

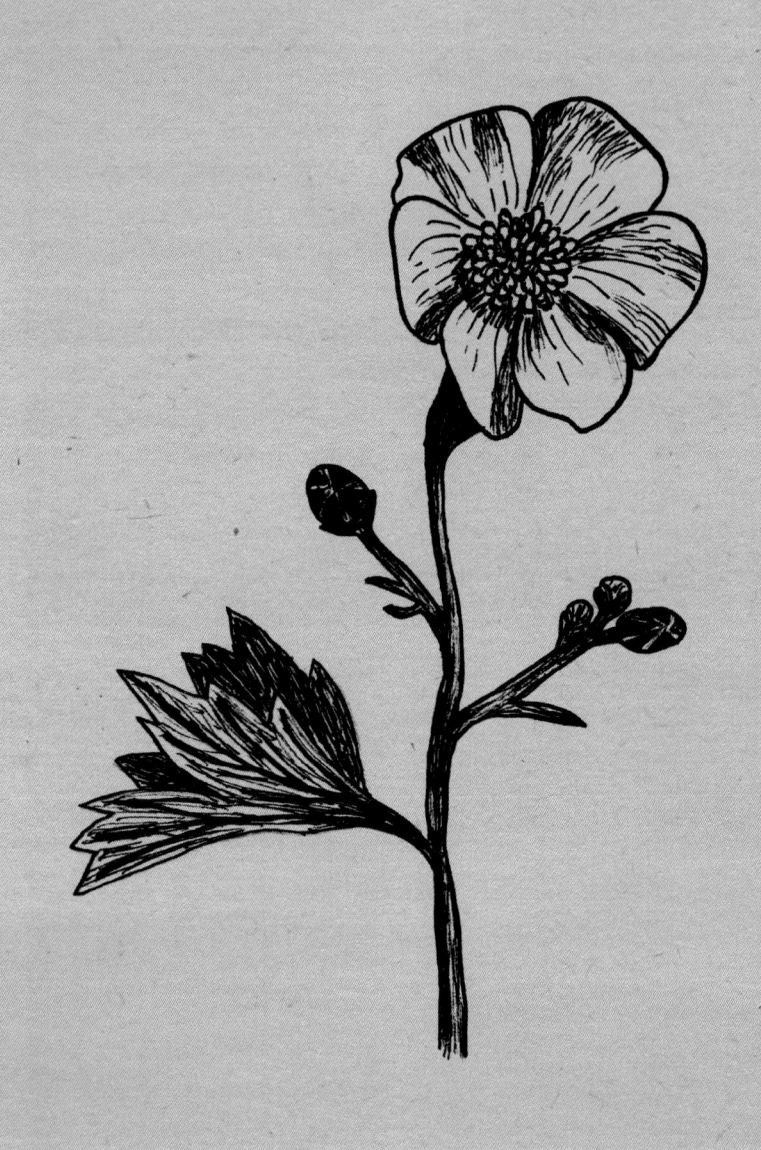

BUTTERCUP

"Oh, I love this song," my mom said as her right hand released the steering wheel of our sky blue Oldsmobile, and she reached down to turn the volume up on the car radio.

I listened intently for a few moments before recognizing the song. It was *Build Me Up Buttercup* by the Foundations.

"This was the first forty-five I ever bought," she continued.

"How old were you back then?" I asked.

"About twelve. Same as you now."

I appreciated that my mom offered up that little tidbit about herself. At that point, I didn't know much about her childhood, besides she grew up Catholic in Oxford, Massachusetts. Both of her parents were alcoholics, and there was never much food in the house. Her best friend, Teresa, lived next door, and Teresa's mom, Irene, loved my mom and took care of her as much as she could.

"I'd show up at Teresa's house most mornings before elementary school because I knew Irene would feed me pancakes," my mom said as she adjusted her silver wire glasses on the bridge of her nose.

I imagined my mom as a kid, sitting at a table with her neighbors, her round young face sticky with maple syrup and framed by her blonde locks. Her belly full and satisfied.

On the days she didn't eat breakfast with the neighbors, she'd eat paste at school.

"It was minty and delicious," was all she'd say about it.

"Now we know what's wrong with us," my siblings and I joked with each other, "Mom was eating whatever horrible chemicals were in paste back in the early sixties."

Mom recounted how her father always told her and her two younger sisters, "Get in the car—let's go get some ice cream." But always, without fail, the catch was that once the girls got their vanilla soft serve, they would stop at the tavern on the way home. My grandfather would go inside and drink "the hard stuff" for hours while my mom and her sisters stayed in the car all night.

"The drunk men would come out of the bar, stumbling around and slurring their words. Oh, it was horrible," my mom told us a million times, "They would try to get us to open the car door by waving bags of chips at us through the window." That scared the shit out of her.

My mom's parents had a tumultuous relationship, full of break-ups and reunions. During one particularly rough split when my mom was about nine, my grandmother took all the kids and moved into an old apartment above a laundromat and a corner store. One night, after everyone had gone to bed, my mom heard someone walk up the staircase to their front door and rattle the doorknob, trying to get inside.

"I slept with a knife under my pillow after that," she'd tell us, "Even after my parents got back together and we moved back into the house."

But as much as my mom spent much of her childhood afraid, she was also a badass.

When she was about thirteen, she and her older brother were ditching school or church, I can't remember which, and a priest saw them walking around. When she and the priest locked eyes, he gave my mother a nasty, shaming look and shook his finger at her in disappointment.

The Scorpio indignation burned bright red like embers inside her, and without breaking eye contact, she flipped the priest off and yelled, "Sit and rotate!" with disgust and defiance in her voice.

Growing up, my best friend Tasia and I adored this story of my mom, and we loved to imagine our heroine rejecting judgment and shame from some stuck-up old priest.

My mom's parents finally divorced when she was fourteen, and she and her dad moved out west to Vancouver, Washington, while her mom and younger sisters stayed behind. I never really knew why and didn't ask any questions until I got older. Like way older. I was in my thirties.

"Well, my dad and I came home one day to an empty house. We had no idea where my mom or sisters were. All that was left on the counter was a box of rat poison," my mom said, "Basically, we took that as her way of telling us to fuck off and die."

That era of my mom's history is filled with a lot of holes and blurry reflections, but another story that eventually surfaced was that my mom was so enraged and hurt by her mother's abandonment that when she found out where her mother was living, she stole a candlestick and in the darkness of night, when nobody would see or catch her, she wrote the word CUNT across all her mother's window screens with the wax.

"That shit doesn't come off," my mom said, not trying too hard to stifle a laugh.

The older I got, the more I poked and prodded her for more stories.

They got darker.

"Auntie Claire said she remembers our mom throwing me down so hard onto the couch as a newborn that I bounced off the cushion and landed on the hardwood floors."

I cried when my mom told me that.

"Why are you crying?" she nervously brushed her hand over the velvety brown armrest of her sofa.

"Because you were so small and helpless, and you didn't deserve that," I said, not with anger for my grandmother in my voice, but with soft compassion for my mother, "I'm so sorry that happened to you."

My mom's cobalt blue eyes filled with tears, and it only took a few seconds for one to roll all the way down her cheek and land on the grey long-sleeve henley she was wearing. It was the one I gave her for Christmas with the creeping buttercups embroidered in a beautiful pattern cascading toward her bustline. Those winding green vines and butterscotch-hued blooms traced the delicate white rivers of her chest, and in that moment they became a symbol of the love and nourishment she gave to my siblings and me, even though she didn't receive these things from her own mother.

For so many years, whenever *Build Me Up Buttercup* came on the radio while I was driving, I'd turn it up and think of my mom as a 12-year-old girl, scraping up some cash to buy her first record—a little something to bring her some joy—and it always made me smile.

But at some point, when my mom's hair turned fully white, and I was just starting to grapple with my own mortality in new and unexpected ways, I was driving down the road and my mom's song came on the radio. My right hand released the steering wheel, I reached down to turn the volume up, and I thought, *Someday I'm going to play this at my mother's funeral.*

And at that moment, *Build Me Up Buttercup* changed forever.

It no longer reminded me of the fresh opportunities of youth. The promise of what could be and the triumphs of what might come, but instead it was a reminder of the ever-forward march of time. That someday, I wouldn't be able to call my mom on the phone with a situation that's got me down, and hear her say to me, "You know what? That bitch isn't as nice as everyone thinks she is."

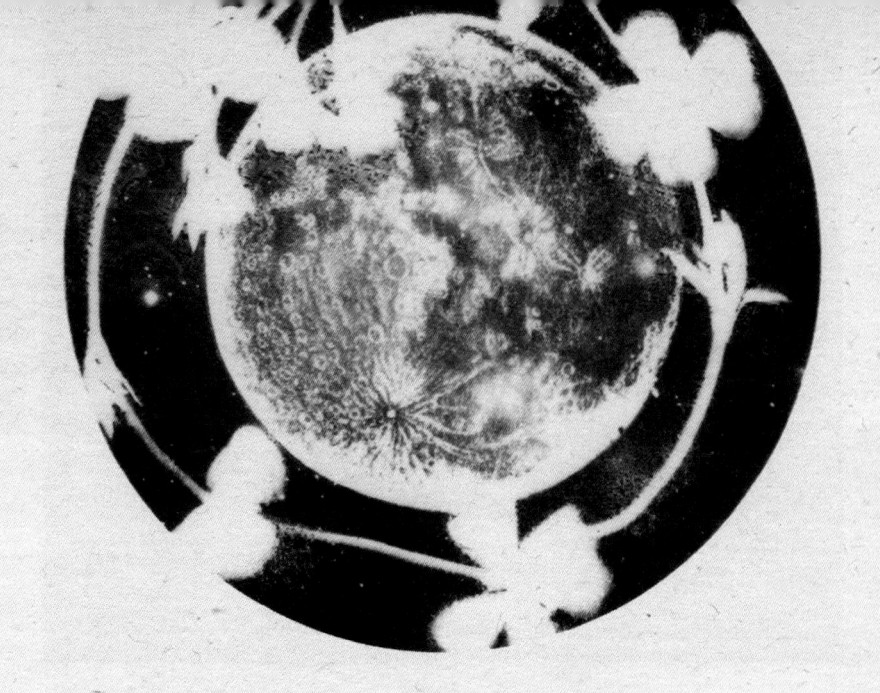

A RITUAL TO REMIND YOURSELF THAT YOU'RE THE BADDEST BITCH

GATHER
- A journal or notebook
- A pen or pencil
- 20-40 minutes
- Your favorite way to create a playlist for yourself, whether that's with an app on your phone or computer, or something more old school like a burned CD or mixed tape.

Think about some of the most potent ways music has shifted the energy in your life, and how powerful and connected to your magic you felt. What would these moments look and feel like if they were music videos?

Give your mind permission to luxuriate in the tastes, textures, and images you conjure up. Set your timer for ten minutes and explore these experiences in your journal in a way that feels good to you.

Now it's time to create a playlist that helps you tap into the core of everything you've just expressed—a playlist that reminds you that you're the baddest bitch of your own life.

Reset your timer for ten minutes and write down a list of songs in your journal that help you celebrate your humanness and connect you to your higher, infinite self. Think of this part of you as your true essence that exists in another dimension. You can't see them, but you're still connected through time and space. You know they are there and they love you beyond all reason. Bring this part of you to mind as you make your list. If you're feeling called to do so, put on some music to help shake off any cobwebs and anchor into this exercise even further.

The only rule to follow when building your playlist is that no toxic positivity is allowed. If you think a song should make you feel good but falls short and makes you feel ashamed of being an imperfect human, it doesn't make the cut.

Anytime you listen to this playlist, take yourself outside if you can. Remember that walking around your neighborhood or outside your workplace during a break can be just as potent as a planned hike on your favorite trail. While outdoors, pay extra close attention to the sky, animals, plants, and humans you meet. Say "thank you" aloud to any affirmations you receive.

If you need help getting started, here are a handful of my favorites from my Baddest Bitch playlist. Feel free to take what resonates, and leave the rest.

FEELING GOOD by Nina Simone
During this song, focus on the sensations that arise in your body as you drop into the present moment and really listen. The intro is just Nina's gorgeous earthy voice serenading the natural world. No instrumentation. Just her third chakra ringing out to the birds, the sun, and the breeze like a hypnotic set of otherworldly windchimes. What does anticipation feel like in your body? By the time she gets to the lines ...*It's a new dawn. It's a new day. It's a new life for me and I'm feeling good*... there's a beautiful, mischievous brassiness in her voice. That's when the bass, strings, keys, and drums finally kick in, creating a crescendo of *fuck yes* and oh my god—her voice turns into a full-on confident swirl of incense smoke and witchcraft. What does power feel like in your body? What about freedom? What do you notice most when you're connected back into the earth and your own damn self?

CAN YOU GET TO THAT by Funkadelic
Time to find your swagger. Allow the luscious fat-bottomed drums, smooth vocals, and groovy rhythm free your body to do whatever the hell it wants for three minutes.

SMOOTH SAILIN' by Leon Bridges
Imagine you're singing this song to yourself, and dream about what smooth sailing would look like for you over the next few weeks.

LOVELY DAY by Bill Withers
As you listen to this song, focus on each beautiful detail of the natural world around you. Pay attention to the small details of the trees. The color of the grass. The shape of the clouds above you. The smell of the flowers. The sound of the rain. The rush of fresh air on your skin. As this song

fades out, notice the ways you feel different from when the song first started.

TIME IS ON MY SIDE by Irma Thomas
Irma Thomas brings me to my knees, and I live for it every time. This song takes on a whole new meaning when you sing it as a duet with your higher self. You take the chorus and imagine your higher self singing the verses and bridge to you with nothing but love and feral acceptance in their voice.

DEAD OF WINTER

I woke up bleeding. Just a whisper in the morning, but it grew into a deafening drone as the day dragged on.

I felt an ash grey fog envelop me.

The sweet smell of butter and sugar wafted from the oven in our little yellow kitchen like the repulsive industrial smokestacks that jut up from the paper mill in the town I grew up in.

This was our third loss in fourteen months.

I sat down at our straw colored dining table to decorate Christmas cookies with Nattie, twenty years old with long brown hair and the spark of aspiration in her pretty blue eyes. She was on winter break from community college and had the day off from her part-time job at Ulta Beauty. She still lived at home. Still loved Christmas.

I didn't tell her I was bleeding. Instead, I pretended it was just another Sunday afternoon.

I tried to wrap my head around royal icing and our meager collection of white jimmies, green sanding sugar, and this miscarriage bleeding out of me, thick and wet and warm.

It might be a subchorionic hematoma.

That happened the last time I was pregnant. On our second wedding anniversary, I sat on the toilet and bright red blood appeared in the water. I was seven weeks along.

Ryan and I rushed to the hospital and saw a heartbeat for the first time in the emergency room ultrasound lab.

I held Ryan's hand, and we squeezed each other in disbelief. Not all was lost.

"The hematoma might heal on its own, or it might get worse and you'll miscarry. It's about a fifty-fifty shot," the ER doctor told us. The bleeding stopped a few days later, and I felt hopeful. I kept envisioning the blood sack between the placenta and my uterus shrinking.

A few weeks after that, at our first prenatal appointment, it was deja vu to the year before.

They couldn't find a heartbeat.

I had very recently miscarried.

There was death inside me.

And now this.

I think most people think a miscarriage is just another period that's instantly swept away with the wave of a magic wand. Like that person was never pregnant in the first place. Or that's what people *wish* miscarriages were. Our patriarchal culture dictates that a pregnant person is allowed to be a little sad, because if they weren't sad at all, they'd be a monster. But they also can't be too sad because then they're overreacting and dramatic. Then the world insists that life must go on immediately, as if nothing traumatic happened at all.

"It could've been so much worse," they say.

"At least it happened early on."

Or worse yet, "They say everything happens for a reason."

This is the absolute worst thing to hear in the midst of anything painful or disappointing. The debasing nature of these words instantly turns my blood into thick fiery lava that gets so hot it glows red and bubbles inside my veins.

I know most folks are just trying to make me feel better. We've all been socialized to offer advice and fixing instead of loving presence when it comes to the brutal parts of life. But knowing this doesn't change the fact that some tragedies will utterly tear you apart, making each unsolicited opinion and platitude a sharp grain of salt rubbed into a raw and aching wound that desperately needs to hear, "You're safe to feel your pain with me."

The other thing most people don't seem to understand is that hormones shift rapidly all over the place when a body goes from being pregnant to not pregnant. And with a miscarriage, those hormones are mixed with shattering grief. It's a dizzying, painful experience, like being completely sucked into a vat of black sticky sludge.

Hope was exhausting, and I was already drained from all the unexpected bleeding the year brought.

Sitting in our dining room decorating holiday cookies, I wished I could completely disintegrate into the dense grey fog, rise up through the rafters in my attic, dissipate into the cold, soggy December air, and rain back down in the new year.

My friend Chris happened to call me three days later, and when he asked how I was doing, I told him exactly what was going on.

"I'm in a really dark place," I sobbed into the phone, the words barely escaping me, "I feel so devastated—like I've lost all my magic to make anything I desire happen anymore."

I've known Chris for twenty years, and even though he was 1,773 miles away in Kansas City, I could hear his whole body soften as I spoke my truth. His gentle witnessing in that moment was a testament to all we've been through together.

"Beets, I'm so fucking sorry. This is so terrible and unfair, and I love you so much," he said, nothing but love and unwavering kindness in his voice.

That day I questioned everything I'd wanted and worked for the previous five years.

I sat on the hardwood floors of my bedroom with the door shut, surrounded by festive rolls of red, green, and blue wrapping paper. The hot pink tape dispenser and a pair of scissors within an arm's reach.

I cut a sheet of paper and laid a box on top of it.

What if I can't have a baby with Ryan?

I wrapped the paper around the box and taped the edge down.

What if I'm a hack and I can't finish writing my book? What if I finish it, and it sucks, and nobody wants to read it?

I folded the ends into neat triangles and secured them

with tape.

What if no matter what I do or work towards, life just dishes out toil and stale crumbs and stop signs from here on out?

I wrote FROM: SANTA on a paper tag with a large pinecone printed on it, then taped it to the front of the wrapped package.

What if my magic is gone forever?

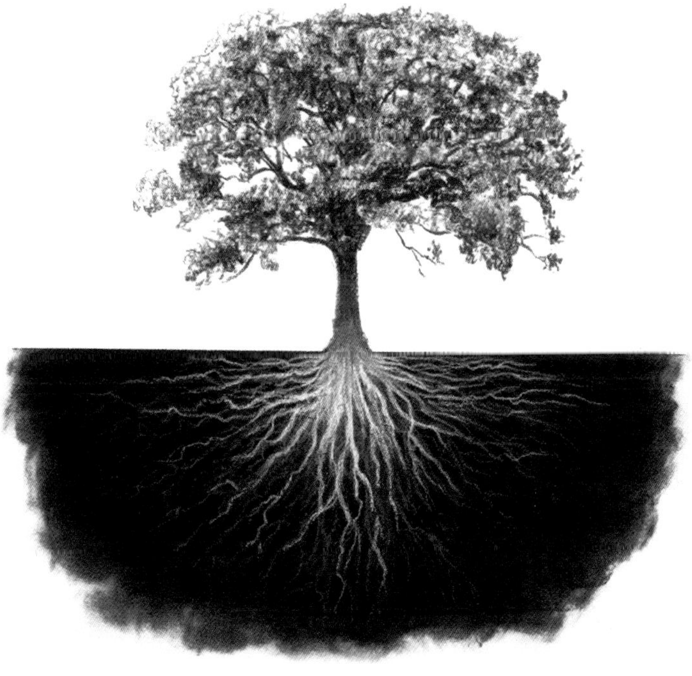

THE OWL

After the third miscarriage, a large tangled knot of grey and black threads formed in my core and completely blocked out every last drop of golden yellow light pulsating from the wise orb in my center.

My womb moved back into an echo chamber of grief. Just like the year before, I stopped ovulating, and my cycles became irregular and elongated. When the thick red rivers finally arrived, they flowed relentlessly from my body, their currents swift and dangerous and messy.

In late March, Ryan and I headed into the woods on the dry side of Oregon, south of The Dalles, where the grey-barked oaks and the red towering ponderosa pines reach up towards fluffy white clouds passing through the blue skies. We were on a mission to completely dissolve into the landscape and soak up the glorious silence.

The woods are always full of magic, even when they're ordinary woods, filled with nothing but raven calls and the scent of pine needles floating through the air. When I'm sick of the city and its harsh lights and endless syncopated clamoring, I crave the forest. When my head is fat and swollen like a wet rag, I need the trees to wring it out.

Emptied.

As we arrived at camp, the tiniest, driest white flakes floated down from the sky.

"It's snowing," Ryan grinned as he got out of our old silver truck. He stretched his arms out above his head and arched his back. His midwestern roots always shined in the coldest weather.

"Do you think it'll stick?" I asked him, stepping out of the truck. I took in a deep breath of clean, fresh air.

"Nah. It's melting as soon as it touches the ground."

We got to work setting up our tan canvas tarp off the back of the truck. Once it was pulled tight over the poles and secured to the ground with stakes, we admired our little porch.

"You want some tea?" I asked.

"Yes, please. If you make the tea, I'll set up our bed."

"Deal."

I wrangled our camping table into position. It's always such a cantankerous affair to set up because the push tabs in the metal legs are so stiff. They were extra hard to handle with cold fingers, but after I worked up a sweat getting the table in order, I placed our forest green camp stove on top, attached the little propane tank, and lit the flame on the burner. While our kettle of water warmed up on the stove, I put two bags of herbal tea into each of our thermoses.

As I poured the boiling water, the sweet smell of lemon, ginger, and rooibos wafted up in the steam.

Ryan walked up behind me, put his arms around my waist, and rested his head on my shoulder. "Oooh, that smells good."

"You smell good," I leaned my head back into the crook of his neck.

He squeezed me a little tighter and said, "Are you ready to get into our nature disguises and go sit still for a while?"

"You know I fucking am," I said, and we both laughed.

We changed into our camouflage coats and pants, pulled our earth-toned beanies over our ears, grabbed our tea, and began walking into the woods. After about a mile, we bushwacked it to the edge of a field where the sky was vast, and we sat, arms and thighs touching, waiting for dusk.

A miracle happens when you sit still, silent, and invisible in the woods.

You become a tree.

That evening, when the world finally shifted into a thousand shades of monochromatic stoney blue, I whispered softly, "This is the time of day when my eyes start playing tricks on me."

"Oh, I know," Ryan whispered back, acknowledging the psychedelic threshold where daytime meets the night.

As soon as those words left Ryan's lips, a silver barred owl appeared in the sky, silent and gorgeous, flying towards us. She landed on the very top of a tall ponderosa pine about forty yards away and peered curiously our way.

"She sees us," Ryan whispered. I nodded ever so slightly, not making any sudden or drastic moves.

I stared into the owl's round mirror face with wonder.

"Who looks for you? Who holds the clue?" she asked.

Did I just hear that right?

I cocked my head, my left ear facing her a little more, and concentrated on listening.

"Who looks for you? Who holds the clue?" she asked again.

My mind, completely blank, suddenly formed one clear thought.

It's time to visit your grandmother.

The silver owl bobbed her head up and down and around in a clockwise circle before she spread her soundless wings and took flight, a grey ghost gliding over the icy dusk air until she disappeared into another patch of tall trees.

THE GARDEN

When I was a small, round song sparrow, and my days were filled with the joy of exploring my expansive, young imagination, sometimes my mom and I would visit my Grandma Mary after lunch. Grandma Mary was my dad's mother, but ever since my parents met when my mom was just fourteen, Mary was my mom's only mother, too.

If we were lucky, my mom and I would find Mary outside, tending to her flowers, pruning the emerald green bushes, and collecting blossoms for her vase. Her long silver hair either braided in one long rope swinging down her back or wrapped around her head in milk braids, each beautiful strand glimmering in the sun.

There were so many tall rows of plants in her garden. Many of them towered over me, and it seemed there was a real possibility they could envelop me completely. This thought thrilled me, and I loved imagining what adventures my grandmother's flower friends would take me on.

I could tell Mary felt at home outside among her roses, lilies, and irises. She moved with ease around her garden, and her deep brown eyes overflowed with life while she tended to her flowers. While she and my mother talked about grown-up things, I closed my eyes and let my mind dance with the intoxicating aromas of stamen and stem warming in the fresh spring air. My grandmother willed these blooms into existence, and I felt her magic in every sweet note they sang.

Sometimes I still visit my grandmother in her garden. It's peaceful there. Just the two of us, the sun shining down on our faces, listening to the sounds of the gentle Washington wind with the *chick-a-dee-dee* birdsong on its wings.

She always welcomes me with a smile, and I ask her so many questions.

What did you write about when you were alive?

What inspired you to channel the deceased spirit of Edgar Rice Burroughs?

Can you tell me everything you know about astrology?

What were some of your favorite conversations you had with plants?

It had been quite a while since I'd trekked to my grandmother's garden, and I couldn't shake the message I received from the barred owl in the woods. It was time to pay Grandma Mary a visit.

When I emerged from behind the big cottonwood tree with the old rope swing hanging down from its thickest branch, I walked across the grass until I saw the top of my grandmother's head in the middle of her garden.

She sat in an old aluminum lawn chair wrapped with pink and peach webbing, waiting for me. When she saw me, she smiled and patted the seat of the empty lawn chair next to her. As soon as I sat down, she reached over to the little table on the other side of her and handed me a crystal tumbler of herbal sun tea.

"Thanks, grandma," I grasped my cup and felt cool droplets of condensation press against my hand.

"You're welcome," she raised her glass. I met her glass with my own, and our cups tinked together in a tiny cheers.

I took a sip of my grandmother's brew and felt the cool mint and fresh citrusy lemon balm wash over my tongue. The earthy aftertaste of calendula bloomed in the back of my mouth as I swallowed.

"This is delicious," I said, leaning back in my chair.

"Thank you. It's my mother Nellie's recipe, and I've been making it since I was a little girl. These were her crystal cups, too. You know that Peace Lily cutting your parents propagated and gave to you and Ryan? Their plant came from a cutting Nellie propagated and gave them when they were first married," she paused and turned her head to look at me, "Did you know that Nellie is a powerful protector in your life?"

I smiled, taking in the good news that I had Nellie's love and support.

"I didn't know that, grandma, but I'll take all the protection I can get."

"I'm just finishing up my break," Mary said, "but I was wondering if you'd like to help me in the garden today?"

"Sure."

Mary handed me a pair of gloves and some shears. I pinched them into my left armpit, held out my hands, and helped Mary out of her lawn chair. Then I followed her over to a long row of red, pink, and yellow roses.

"I'm just removing the spent blooms from these today," she said.

"Ok, I can help with that." I nodded at Mary, and we got to pruning.

After I trimmed off a particularly huge faded and shriveled light pink rose with a satisfying, clean snip, I stopped to watch Mary work, admiring her wise hands handling her shears as if they were an extension of her own body.

That's when she stopped deadheading her roses and faced me.

"You know, Christine, when I was a little girl living in Canada, I was the oldest student at Ponoka County Rural School. And one of my jobs was to arrive each day before anyone else—even the teacher—and light all our lamps and get the fire going in the old pot-bellied stove."

"That's pretty impressive," I said, "My fire-building skills still need work, and I'm almost forty years old."

Mary laughed, then continued, "Yes, I quite enjoyed it. It gave me some time to be alone with my thoughts each day."

Murph hopped by and nudged her nose into my leg. She stood up on her hind legs, so I crouched down closer to the damp earth and scratched behind her ears. I brought her here the day she died, when she was scared and sick. She and grandma keep each other company.

"One morning, after I lit the fire in the stove, I saw strange and beautiful visions in the flames," Mary continued, "I saw a black-haired girl and thought she was my future daughter. After that day, I always dreamed of giving birth to a black-haired little girl. My black-haired child turned out to be your dad, though."

She paused for a moment, looking into my eyes before she said, "Who I saw that morning all those years ago was actually *you*."

Ice cold shock poured over my head and down my entire body.

"What exactly did you see, grandma?" I asked, as nervous and excited energies bloomed pink and wild inside my chest.

"Well, it was so peculiar. As soon as I lit the fire, I saw your face inside the stove. You were about twelve, just like me. You reached your hand out, and as soon as I put my hand in yours, we started floating off the ground. Before I knew it, we were above the old school house, gently drifting higher and higher into the sky.

We kept ascending, pushing past the Earth's atmosphere further and further until our feet touched down on the moon's soft, dusty surface. As we stood there in awe, looking back at the blue and white marble we just came from, the crater we stood in began to tremble beneath us. That's when the moon swirled and shifted into an enormous, beautiful silver barred owl."

My mouth hung open as I listened in awe to Mary's vision, goosebumps pushing out from the skin in my arms and legs.

"We weren't scared," Mary continued, "We just held hands as we rode on the back of the silver owl through our solar system. I'll never forget the golden hues of Venus or the vertical rings around Uranus. The further we traveled from home, the colder it became. We passed by Pluto and more large frozen rocks.

Five trillion miles from Earth, we blasted into interstellar space, where we sat in awe, staring at billions of suns with their own planets and moons. But only a few moments after we arrived, the silver owl screeched, and we burst into a tunnel of pindot lights as we accelerated through time and space. When we finally stopped, we were in the nebula of Orions's dark cloud. Oh, Christine, we couldn't believe our eyes! Those purple and lavender gas and dust clouds were so much more beautiful than anything we'd ever seen! The owl flew us inside, and we all watched so many tiny stars being born in this celestial hatchery."

"That's incredible—what happened next, grandma?" I asked, eyes wide.

"Then we left the Milky Way entirely. We entered into the vast black expanse between galaxies—intergalactic space. There, we witnessed thin whips of gas. Dark matter. Stray dust. It was so desolate and freezing cold. But it didn't matter how cold it got on our journey because we could still feel the warmth from the fire back at the schoolhouse.

The owl let out another screech, and a burst of speed led us down a wormhole. We heard static in our ears as a storm of green and purple light whipped all around us. We were eighty billion trillion light years from home when we finally stopped moving. We made it to the end of the universe, where we witnessed the beginning of everything. With every ounce of its energy densely packed into the tiniest point, we observed this ticking timebomb explode with such a force that it created and propelled endless

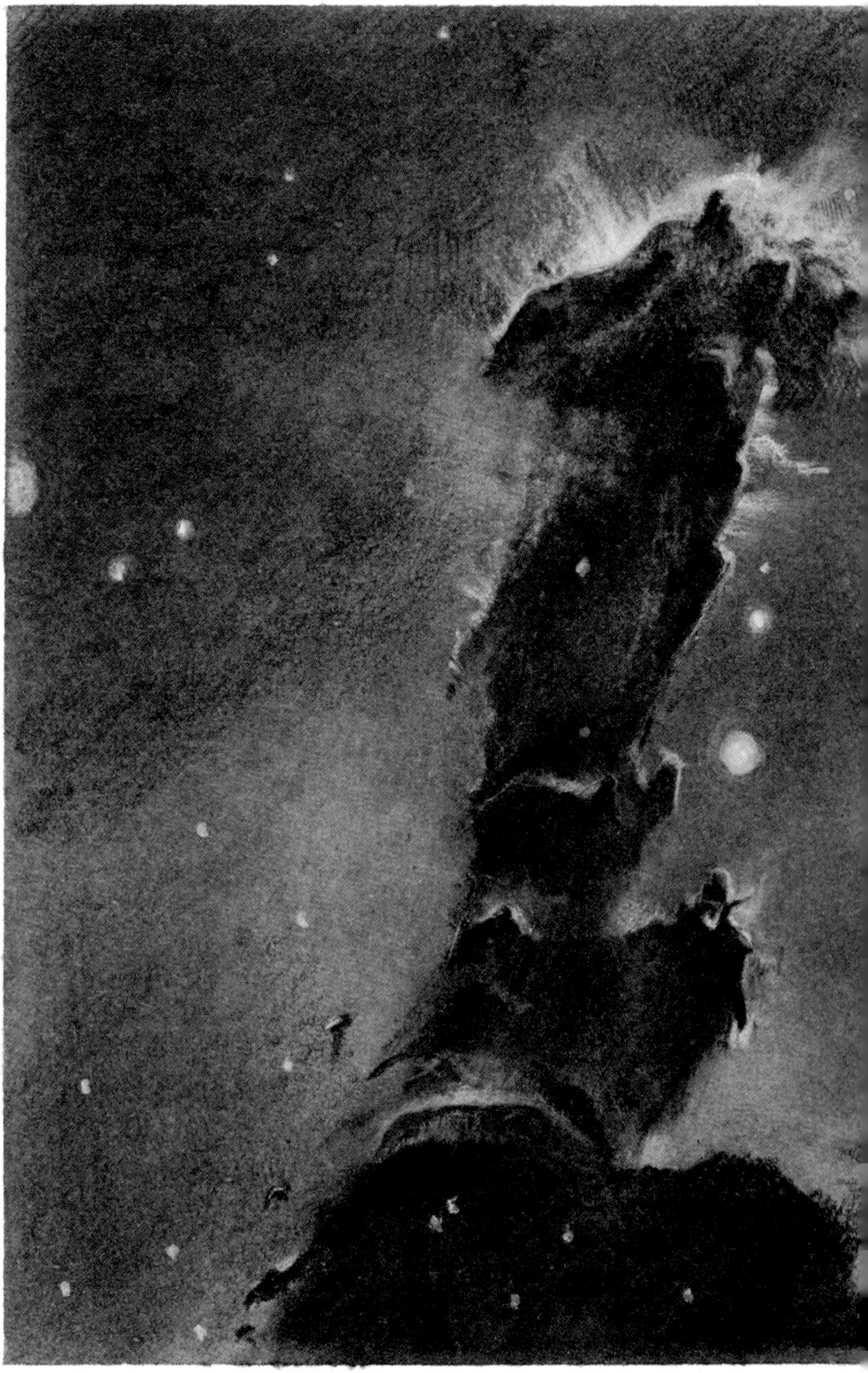

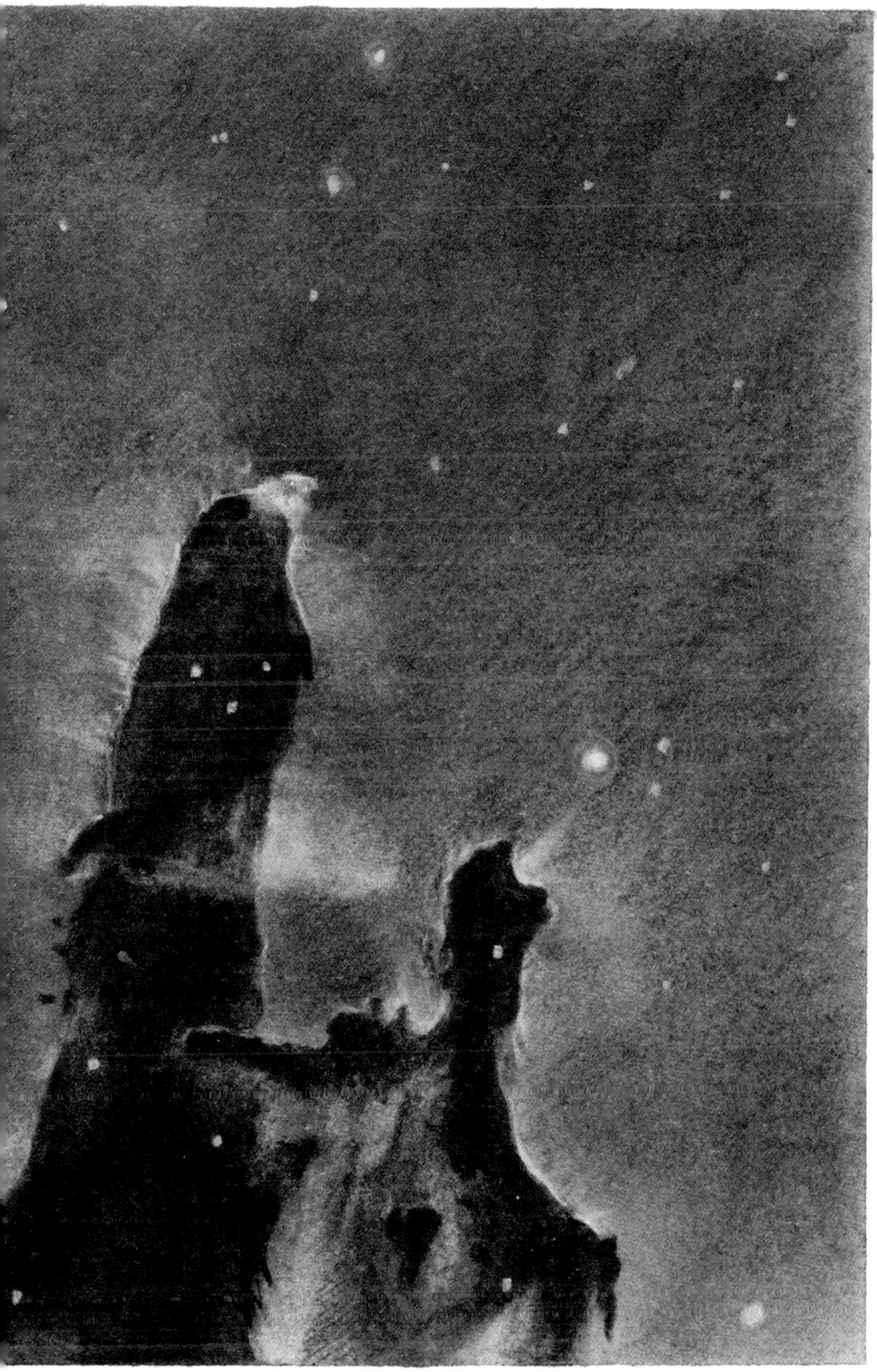

matter outward to make the billions of galaxies of our vast universe."

Mary noticed all the silent tears streaming down my face and reached into her apron pocket. She offered me her white handkerchief. Her initials were embroidered on it in tiny purple stitches.

"Grandma, are you saying that you and I are ancient?" I took the handkerchief from Mary and wiped my eyes and cheeks.

"Yes. And I realized that day, back in the school house, that every living thing is a spark flying out from the origin of the universe," Mary said, "You are as powerful as that explosion because you came from it. That magic is always in you. Always. No matter what."

"You've got a big heart," she continued, placing her hand on my forearm, "You love so deeply. And you feel so deeply. You're creative and inspired. Your energy is strong and sturdy like a giant redwood, with roots so deep in the earth you can gather all you need from the sky. You're a miracle, with billions of other miracles that came before you—and you contain all those miracles inside you."

I opened my arms, embracing Mary in a big hug. A deep, primal sobbing sprang from my core and rushed past my throat as big wet tears exploded from my eyes. My mouth curled into a misshapen potato. This is what most people call ugly crying. The truth, though, is that it's important, beautiful, cleansing alchemy. There's nothing ugly about it.

As I sobbed into my grandmother's shoulder, the thick ball of knotted black and grey threads in my core untangled themselves and made their way out of me, landing on the ground and dissipating into a sparkling silver mist. I could finally feel the orb of golden yellow light pulsating from the wise orb in my center, and as it broke free from all the darkness that held it back for so long, it expanded outward, enveloping my grandmother and me in her beautiful garden.

When I finally pulled away, I wiped my eyes on my grandmother's handkerchief and let out a deep sigh.

"I want to show you something," Mary said as she leaned over and clipped the long stem of an iridescent purple and yellow iris into her hand. "Will you walk with me into those woods over there?" She pointed the iris like a scepter toward a thick wood of towering trees about sixty yards away.

I nodded, and we slowly made our way over there, stepping through tall grasses and patches of warm dirt. With each step further into the forest, I could feel the love of the tree elders around me—their energy thick, calm and wise like the sap that flows through each of them.

The path is unfolding.

The dreams you seek are seeking you.

Watch for miracles—they are coming.

In the distance, my ancient giant redwood with the emerald green wooden door at the base of its broad trunk appeared on the horizon, and more calm washed over me like a warm bath. I knew where we were going.

When we arrived inside my little forest temple, Wolf jumped off the soft bed and greeted us, wagging her tail

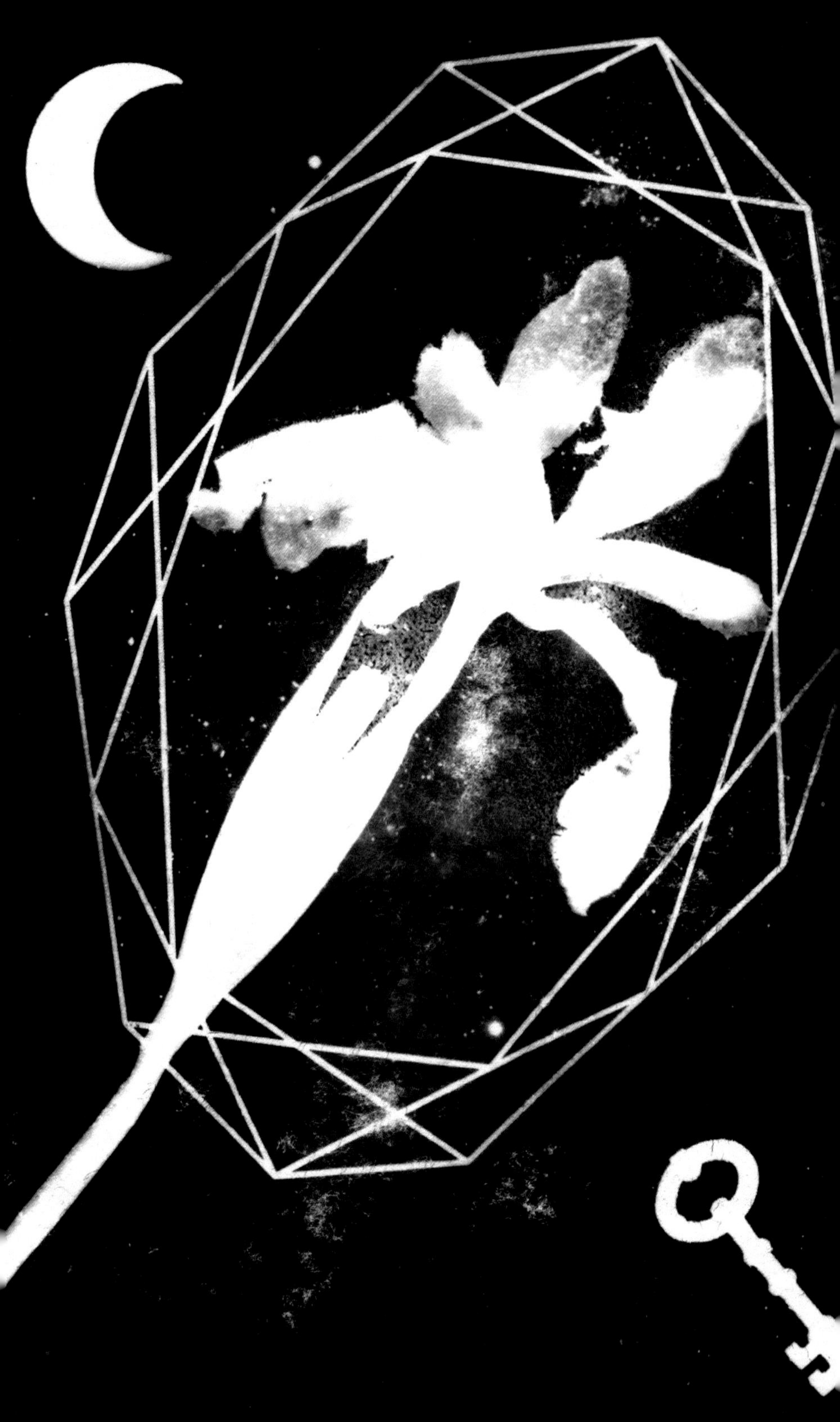

with excitement. I knelt down and patted her strong, soft back and scratched under her chin. Her fur smelled like fresh cold air and fir needles. I took my shoes off and squished my toes into the soft dirt floor, then watched as Mary placed her iris on the altar and lit a candle next to it.

When the room quieted to just the sound of our breath and the fire crackling as it blackened the candle wick, Mary broke the silence.

"There's one last thing I need to tell you. When you feel lost, write a letter to the moon. That's how you reach all the ancestors all at once. We're always there to listen and send our help from the unseen places."

I nodded and took in a slow, relaxed, deep breath, savoring the sweet and earthy smell of the familiar bare redwood walls. Mary hugged me and took my face in her beautiful creased hands.

"I'm so proud of you, and I want all your dreams to come true. We all do," she said softly.

Mary picked up her iris bloom from the altar and handed it to me. "For all the abundance, good fortune, and creative fire," she said, with so much devotion in her loving brown eyes.

I took the bloom in my hand and closed my eyes as I brought it up to my nose and inhaled the intoxicating buttery-soft powder aroma. As it flowed into my nose and dispersed throughout my body, it nestled a little piece of wisdom into my tributaries of blood.

When I grow a new life from a tiny seed and tend to it with love and wonder, Mary is there too. And as my hands start to grow wiser with each passing spring, the difference between me and my time-patinated grandmother shrinks. We were never so separate after all—just two sparks of light from the same flame.

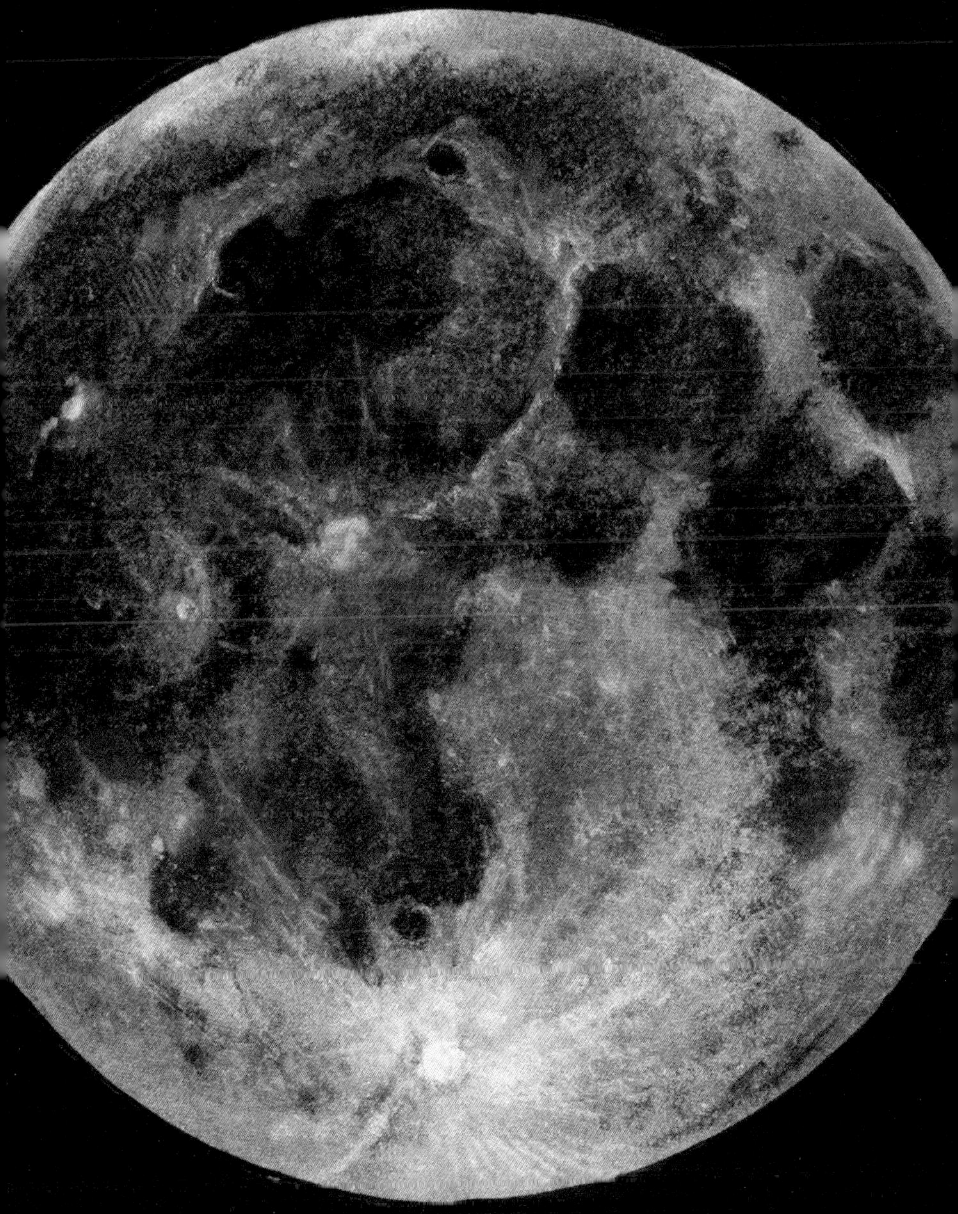

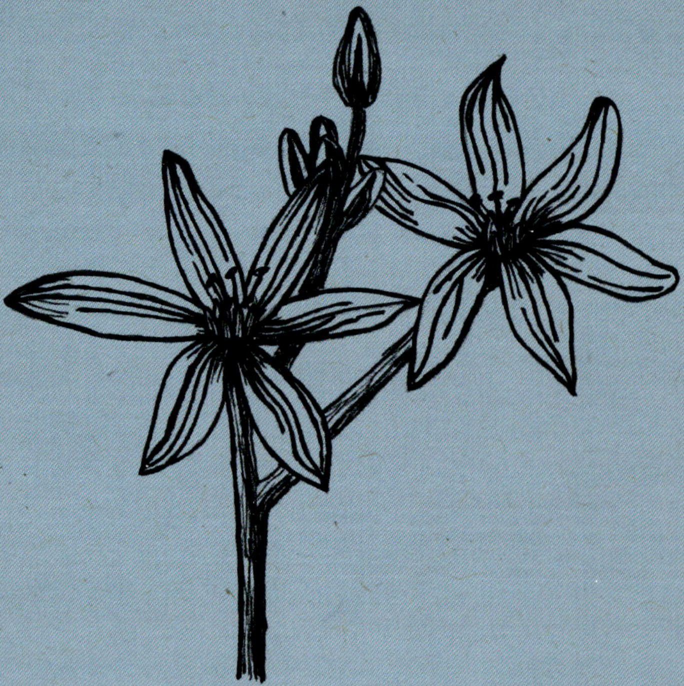

STAR OF BETHLEHEM

Mother moon
Protects us
In her gentle light
Creating
Sacred space.

Unfurl and
Release those
Suffering ghosts
Into the mending
Waters of the
Eternal universe.

You are loved
And supported.

A RITUAL TO CONNECT WITH THE MOON

GATHER
- A comfortable place to sit and look up at the moon. If the moon isn't visible, collect a small object that represents the moon to you.
- A bowl of fresh water
- A piece of paper to write a letter on
- A pen or pencil
- 10-15 minutes

Find a comfortable place to sit, and take your time settling into the space. When you're ready, find the moon in the sky, or hold your moon-like object in your hands, and spend the next few minutes softly gazing into it. Take in all the small details of the moon, and think about the moon as an ancestor. What kind of ancestor are they? What do you want to ask the moon? What does the moon want you to know?

Talk to the moon or write the moon a letter.

If you're talking with the moon, hold your bowl of water below your face so it can catch all of your words.

Keep talking or writing for ten minutes, and don't stop. Don't judge anything that comes up. This correspondence is just between you and the moon. It's ok if it doesn't make any sense or if you surprise yourself. As emotions come up, allow them to communicate their truths through you. The moon is there to witness you and all your feelings with love and empathy.

Once you've wrapped up the last thing you want to say, take a few moments to imagine all the ancestors who have done this before you, and notice what it feels like to be connected to them through the moon.

If you wrote a letter, fold it up and place it in your bowl of water, allowing the water to soak up all of your words.

Place your bowl outside or near a window as an offering to the moon. Before you go to bed, visualize the moon turning into a beautiful silver barred owl. Imagine her flying down all 238,900 miles to your windowsill and drinking some of the water while you sleep, knowing she'll bring your message back with her to share with all the ancestors.

Upon rising the next morning, empty the bowl of water into the earth, and before you start your day, take a few moments to close your eyes and feel all the love and support your ancestors are already sending your way.

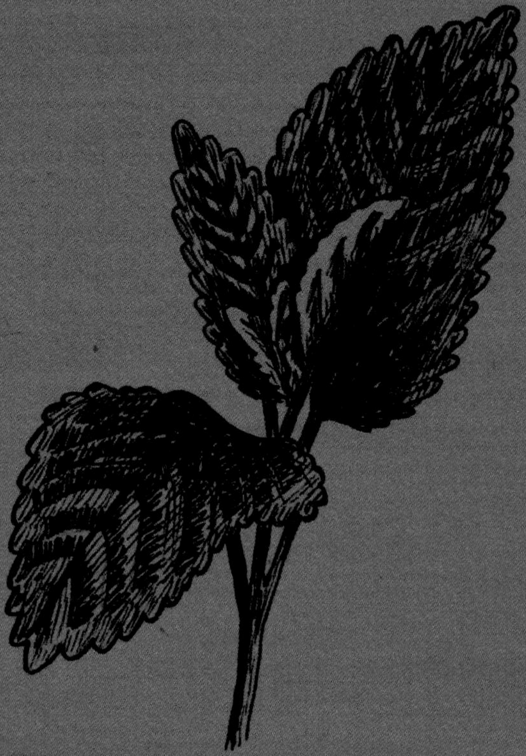

LEMON BALM

"Reset the clock,"
Says the healer,
"And find the truth."
Plunge into a
Soothing pool of
Abundant joy and
Emerge anew.
Radiantly
Steeped in
Glimmering hope.

OVER THE HILL

I thought my life was ending at forty, but it was really just beginning. My biggest regret is not seeing that and going after my dreams.

—Ethel Stark

Dear Mother Moon,

When I was in my twenties, I thought a lot about my late thirties. I had a particular image in my mind about who I'd be and what I'd be up to. It always involved writing my first book and wearing a faux fur leopard print coat paired with bright cherry red lipstick.

And it's always been easy to imagine being a little old witchy lady someday. One who lives out in the woods talking to the plants and who occasionally travels to Reno to play gigs with old friends on a casino stage in our Dolly Parton cover band.

But I never really thought about turning forty. As much as I fight against the patriarchy, I hate to admit that midlife still feels like some big looming deadline.

When Ryan and I started dreaming about having some babies, we always said, "We'll be done by the time Christine turns forty." And that plan didn't pan out. In fact, it ruthlessly blew up in our faces. These struggles still aren't behind us. And that pain is still something I grapple with. Something I'm still working through.

I also know the ending to this story isn't written yet.

So today, after four decades, my wish is that being "Over the Hill" means gaining some smooth momentum after a steep slog.

That it means more of enjoying the view and the breeze and sunshine on my face.

That it means ease.

The patriarchy wants me to believe this milestone is the end of my life, but I know deep in my bones made of star stuff that's a big fucking lie. I refuse to relinquish my magic and my power. Especially now, as I'm just starting to really understand how much bigger and brighter it can get from here.

Please help me remember this as I step over this threshold into the next chapter of my life.

Love,

Christi

A RITUAL TO CREATE THE FUTURE OF YOUR DREAMS

GATHER
- A safe place outdoors with direct sunlight for 2-3 hours where you can leave a pitcher of tea unattended. If you don't have access to an outside space, a window inside your home with direct sunlight streaming into it for 2-3 hours will work just as well.
- Lemon balm - either a handful of fresh leaves or 1 Tbsp. dried
- Peppermint or spearmint - either a handful of fresh leaves or 1 Tbsp. dried
- Calendula - either a handful of fresh flowers or 1 Tbsp. dried
- A large loose leaf paper tea filter or clean drawstring muslin bag
- A large glass pitcher with a lid
- A large serving spoon or wooden spoon
- Fresh drinking water
- Your favorite glass or mug
- Ice (optional)
- Notebook or journal
- Pen or pencil

Gather your herbs and place them in your paper or cloth tea bag, securing the open end shut. Place it in the bottom of your glass pitcher, and fill the whole thing with cool drinking water. Nestle your pitcher into its sunny spot and take a few moments to ask the sun to infuse your potion with courage, clarity, and creativity.

Allow two to three hours to steep.

When the tea is ready, wash your hands and use your spoon to fish out the tea bag. Gently squeeze out any excess water from the teabag into the pitcher, and thank the plants for their magic and wisdom.

Sip on your brew hot or over ice while you list in your journal all the specific ways you want to show up in your life, your community, and the world with your time, talent, passion, and resources.

Store your pitcher of tea in the fridge, and remember that this is an important seed you've planted today. Pay attention to any new ideas that come up over the coming week that feel like a *hell yes* inside your body. Pour yourself a cup of this tea each day until the pitcher runs out. While you drink your daily potion, come back to your journal for a few minutes to revise and add to your list.

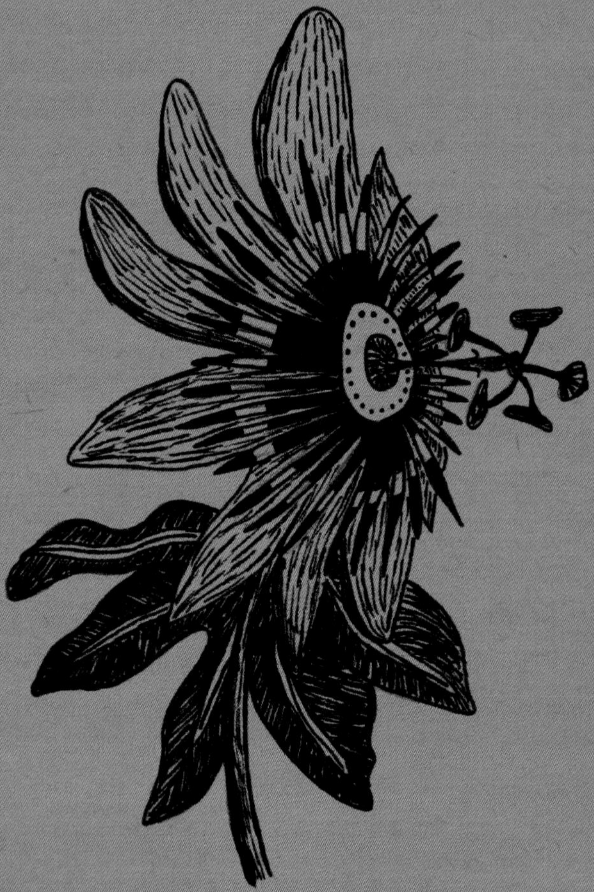

PASSIONFLOWER

Dance with the sun.

Imbibe the sweetness
Within reach.

Rest in the quiet and
Remember who you are.

An easy tempo
Lived willfully
Even for a moment
Brings joy into
Focus.

THE FLOWER SUPERMOON

When spring arrived, and the daylight started to yawn and stretch itself awake, winter's cold, wet grey steadied onward. While everyone I ran into complained about still needing to wear their winter coats every time they left their houses, I soaked up every cool, rainy day, feeling the natural world reflecting myself back to me.

I wasn't quite ready for the bustle that fresh sunshine brings—hikes and camping trips with friends, sitting outside on busy coffee shop patios, or planting the garden.

Instead, I remembered the wildfires from the previous two summers, and I said to the sky, "Give us every last drop you've got. We need it. The tomato starts can wait."

The endless rainfall made everything in my garden lush and green. Slender fuzzy poppy leaves emerged, practically bursting out of the ground. Mounds of tiny fresh lavender foliage sang joyous ballads. Mint, lemon balm, and horehound all shot up toward the sky with the biggest, juiciest leaves I'd ever seen.

Usually, as soon as the garden comes back to life after its winter hibernation, I start harvesting and making plans on what new plants to add and what kind of medicine and magic to create. But I didn't feel like doing any of that. Instead, I soaked up their beauty and gave back in gratitude for all they'd shown and given me.

"How are you doing? What do you need today?" I asked the plants. And then I listened for the answers.

I weeded their beds, their colorful ceramic pots, and the pea gravel pathways surrounding them. I trimmed some of them way back. I sent loving energy their way every chance I got. Ryan and I placed solar-powered fairy lanterns along the fence, hung some up in the thick apple tree branches, and tucked big luminescent crystal balls in the nooks and crannies of the flowerbeds. The magic in our garden was palpable, and in early May, when all the flowers arrived at the same time, everything buzzed with a vitality I'd never seen before.

I didn't pluck any of the ripe blooms. I left them to shine and belt out a chorus of spirited songs. I watched the happy bees collect their pollen, tiny black legs fat with big clumps of bright yellow dust. When the blossoms wilted and faded away, I took my shears and trimmed each one off its stalk with a silent thank you sent psychically through the ether.

Inside the house, I moved the potted Peace Lily to the top of my dresser next to our bed. Half of its long waxy leaves hung over the side, so Nellie could watch over me as I slept.

By the time May's supermoon hung high in the cool night air, my own vibrancy had returned. My whole body sunk into a glowing state, soft and dewy. My womb felt safe and nurtured, and my menstrual cycles shifted back onto the right track.

One night, right at sundown, when Ryan and I were leaning against the chain-link fence, admiring our beautiful garden as the magical golden crystal balls and fairy lights started illuminating one by one, I turned to him and said, "How do you feel about taking the summer off from trying to have a baby? What if instead, I finish writing my book, we get outside as much as possible and get Nattie off to university?"

Ryan looked at me, his sweet face framed by his favorite camo ball cap. It was the one I bought for him with *Sci-Fi Sluts for Reforestation* embroidered on it in a penny-hued thread. His long brown hair nestled into two little buns at the nape of his neck.

He leaned over and kissed my cheek.

"I like that idea," he said, "I'm really not ready to try again. I'm still pretty beat up from the past few years."

I nodded and put my arm around his waist. I leaned my head into his shoulder.

"I love you so much, honey," I said, "Shit's been so hard and there's nobody else I'd rather ride the waves with than you."

"Amen to that," Ryan said, as he put his arm around my shoulder, "You become more amazing every day."

"So do you, my love."

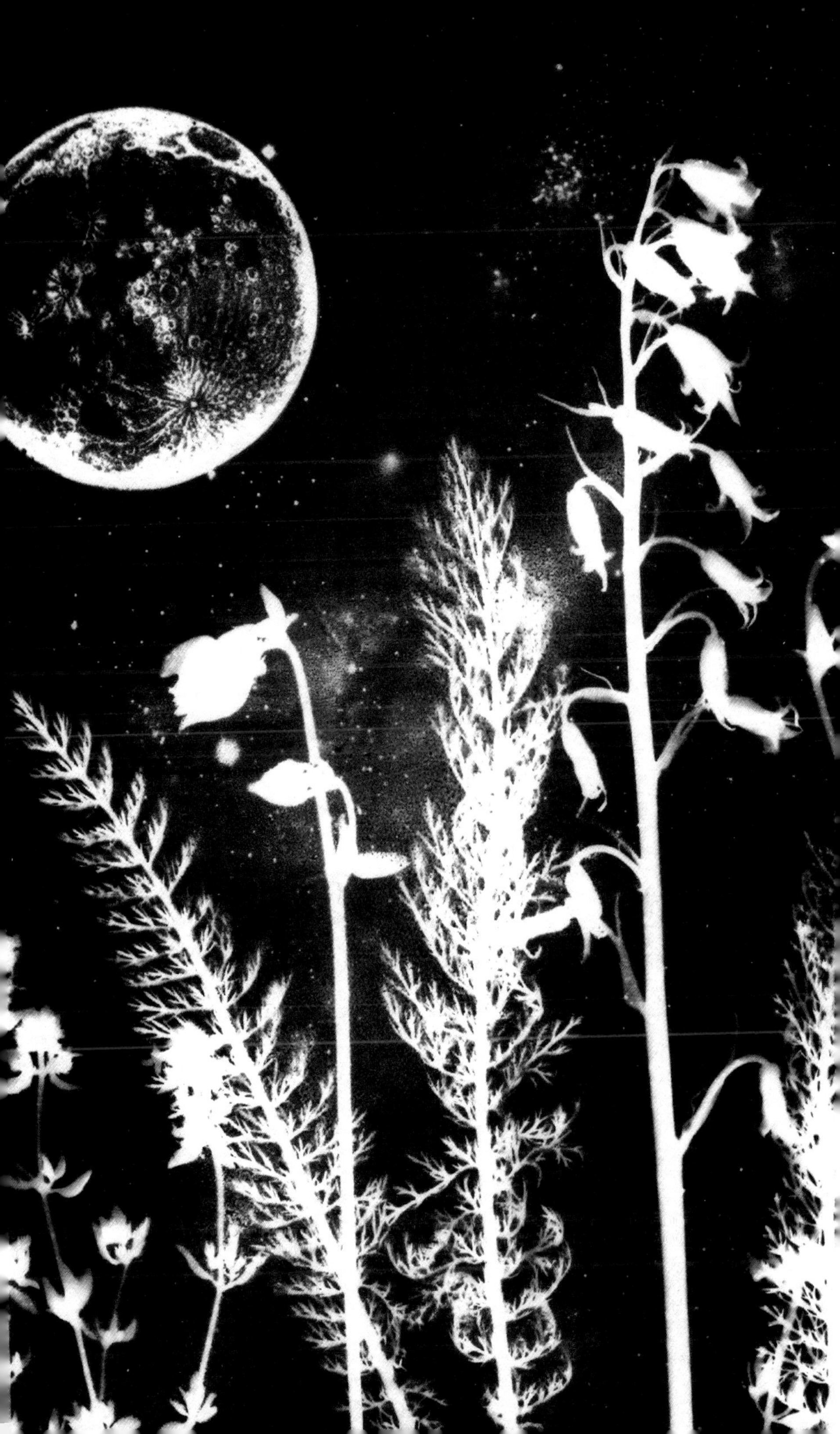

DANDELION

Expand into
Resilience
Guided by the
Sunlight of a
Rich inner world
To call home.

Ground in its
Safety and know
Your truth is
Ancient and
Bright.

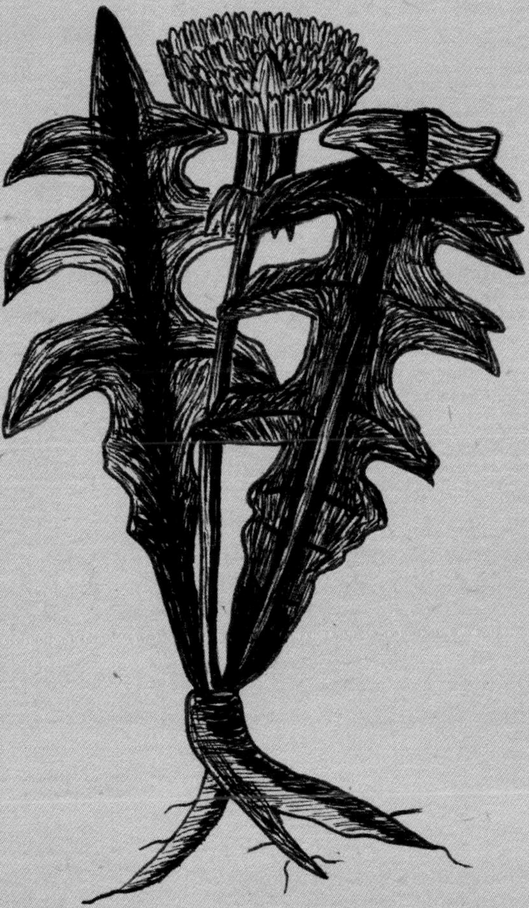

THE OTTER

do what is right for you.
do it over and over again.
lean into the light.

—yung pueblo

I stood in a tiny wood-paneled room on the second story of Central Christian Church, my young body draped in a long white dress. Synthetic floral air freshener swirled around me, getting caught in the delicate white lace veil flowing down my back.

My best friend, Tasia, sat cross-legged on the fluffy beige couch near the window that faced 39th Avenue, her knees forming a tent out of her long, stretchy red dress. It was a beautiful June day, and the gilded sun floated in through the window, catching and illuminating all the dust particles floating around us in that tiny room.

Tasia and I were born just two months apart to two sets of parents who are close friends. We weren't related by blood, but we grew up together. We were chosen family, and she was my Maid of Honor.

Tasia looked over at me, and as soon as I caught her ocean blue gaze, I saw a sparkle in her eye that I'd recognized since we were kids. She unfurled her hand like a water lily, revealing a set of car keys in her palm. They belonged to her older sister, Maria, and they glowed pinkish-white in a beam of the summer sun.

"It's not too late," Tasia said, not breaking eye contact with me, "Don't marry Mark. Let's run away."

For a split second, I wasn't eighteen. I was my infinite self. The patriarchal trappings of shame and unworthiness fell away from me, and I met Tasia's twinkly eyes with a sly smile I knew she was equally familiar with.

"How do we get out of here?" I asked, my voice low.

"Well, first of all, you have to take off those stupid shoes," she said, giggling, "And then we open this window and climb down this fire escape ladder."

I unclasped the little gold buckles around my ankles and slipped out of my shiny white wedding shoes. My clammy feet found an energizing respite on the cool, hardwood floor. I walked over to Tasia and stepped onto the ugly beige couch.

"How do we get this open?" I asked, reaching up to the metal window frame. I gave it a good, hard push, and the window opened with a soft squeak. I climbed into the window and sat on the edge of the sill, my bare feet dangling in the warm air. I took a deep breath in. The air smelled like summer in Portland. Like warm earth and fresh-cut grass and car exhaust.

I stood up on the first rung of the cold black wrought iron fire escape ladder and began my descent down. When my toes finally reached the prickly bark mulch on the ground below, I looked up and saw Tasia peeking out the window, her long brown wavy hair dangling down past her face.

"It's easy!" I reassured her.

"I know," she said, "Catch." She tossed Maria's black tangle of car keys down to me. I missed the catch, but the bark dust stopped their fall with a quiet thud.

After Tasia hopped off the ladder's last rung, I asked, "So, where are we going?"

"Depoe Bay," she said. "Let's watch the sunset over the ocean and celebrate your freedom. But we need to leave a note for Maria first."

We scurried over to Maria's 1986 pearly white Mercedes convertible, parked squarely in the middle of the large church parking lot. With the vintage white drop top down, we hopped inside and rummaged around in the glove box until we found an old receipt and a white pen from Joy Teriyaki with the phrase *You deserve to feel joy* embossed in gold along the barrel.

Tasia scribbled furiously on the receipt. We couldn't find any tape, but Tasia discovered a single piece of gum under the passenger seat. She unwrapped it from its silver foil, then folded the thin pink rectangle slice into her mouth. As she began chewing, she said, "This'll work. I'm going to leave our note on the front door of the church."

Even from the middle of the parking lot, I could hear the sound of two hundred people inside the church bustling around, and suddenly I got nervous. My heart was racing, and I could feel my face begin to flush.

"Ok, hurry up. I'm gonna start the car," I said.

Maria's car purred like a magical panther, and I watched Tasia from the rearview mirror as she approached the front of the church. For the first time ever, I noticed black smoky tendrils swirling around and pulsating from the bricks and under the big wooden door.

How did I miss that before?

Tasia stuck the wad of bubble gum onto the rotten old church and smooshed our receipt note onto it. It stuck!

"Go, go, go!" Tasia said as she slid into the passenger seat.

I shoved the clutch into reverse and got us the hell out of there.

As the freeway led us out of the city and toward the Pacific Ocean, Tasia reached into her bra and pulled out a clove cigarette. She reached down and pushed in the black round lighter in the dash, and when it popped out again, she put the cigarette in her mouth and lit it with the glowing halo nestled inside the shiny metal cylinder.

The smell of warm, spicy smoke filled the air between us.

I looked over at Tasia, and she offered me a drag. I inhaled, but just into my mouth. I wasn't a smoker, but I needed some protection and bright, fearless courage.

I turned on the radio and started flipping through the stations. The sun became brighter in the sky for a moment and suddenly everything was aglow in an apricot sheen. The hiss of radio static surged louder through the speakers for a split second and the quick scent of ozone made me shiver.

"Ooh! Stop there," Tasia heard a song she liked. "This is so weird. I've never heard this song before, but it's oddly familiar."

"Yeah, how do I know all the words?" I laughed.

I turned the shiny black volume knob and blasted the song. We sang as loud as we could into the hot summer air.

Drivin' down I-5
I don't ever wanna die
'Cause I'd no more get to see
All this beauty passin' by me
Laundry on the line
Truckers passin' on the right
Every color on the wind
You know you're livin' if you've sinned
Down I-5

Our magical snow panther followed the asphalt trail all the way to Depoe Bay, and we arrived as the day swelled, voluptuous and pregnant with impending evening energies.

We watched the rainbow sherbet sunset on the beach while we ate clam chowder, creamy and thick, from to-go cups. With every bite, I sunk my bare feet deeper into the sand.

"What's next?" I asked.

"Anything you want."

I watched the glowing pumpkin sun become a sliver on the horizon.

Anything I want?

I handed my empty cup to Tasia and stood up, unearthing my sand-warmed feet. I took off running toward the ocean and felt the wind dancing in my hair.
"Get it, girl!" Tasia called after me.

When I reached the water's edge, I kept going. The rush of the cold Pacific Ocean enveloped my feet.

My shins.

My thighs.

My waist.

I plunged the rest of my body down into the cleansing saltwater of Mother Earth.

"Hello, my dear," the ocean whispered into my ear, "You didn't really run away so much as you ran towards yourself. Don't ever go back."

I felt slippery kelp brush past my knees, and my lungs eventually became hot with stale air.

I popped out of the water and took a deep cleansing breath. I looked down and found my white gown had been replaced by gorgeous, dense velvety fur. The newly-risen moon shone down from the darkening sky, and the moonlight created sparkles on the drops of water beading up on my sable arms.

I dove back into the water and opened my eyes to the boundless blue-green universe. I swam deeper and faster, wriggling my body with ease and watching the moonbeams weave themselves tenderly through the billowing salty kelp forest.

When I reached the kaleidoscope dreamscape of the ocean floor, I watched in awe as the memory of eternity flashed in each purple spiny sea urchin and orange rocky starfish. I saw the ocean blinking back at me, iridescent and holographic, and I felt its heartbeat heading towards me. It reached the tips of my whiskers first, softly making itself known. Then each beat worked its way into my face, rippling through my neck, down my short furry arms and long slender body, until it reached the tip of my long tail and filled every single inch of my body with the ancient rhythm of

I am.

I am.

I am.

I am.

It's the truth of every past and future moment. A reminder that water is the lifeblood of existence. The womb waters of us all. Safe and violent. Familiar and mysterious. Full of both hope and despair.

But it was mostly hope that permeated my heart at that moment.

Hope that love always finds me and fills in the cracks. Hope that I could find it in myself to truly believe that I am enough, exactly as I am. That there's nothing to prove and that vulnerability and authenticity are my biggest strengths.

Water holds the magic of what it means to be alive and a part of the earth.

A few hundred feet away, I spotted a large group of otters headed toward me and I recognized them all. They were my coven. All the souls I go deep with, both in this lifetime and each one that came before.

They swam all around me, protecting me in a luminescent orb of love. Eventually, they encircled me entirely and began weaving a crown of kelp around my head—a nourishing ritual to welcome me home.

One by one, they nudged my face with their little black noses, tickling my face with their white whiskers. Some of them whispered into my ear with loyalty and affection, as they added their piece of kelp to my crown.

"For transformation and love," said Nattie.

"For joy and belonging," said Ryan.

"And for finding magic in the mystery," said the baby I might not ever meet in this lifetime.

It seemed like I could hold my breath down there forever, held in the ocean's embrace. But eventually, I felt her release me, and I kicked my furry flippered feet back through the kelp forest, past the silver coins of fish flying around in their hive mind, until I felt my face reach the night air.

I didn't gasp like I was expecting, but instead, I took another long deep breath, my belly full of wind and light. I floated along the waves on my back for a while, rocking in the undulating maternal swells and listening to the moon tell stories to the twinkling stars—stories about the magic flowers.

I'm never going back.

A RITUAL TO FIND YOURSELF AGAIN

Clear the decks.
Wash your feet.
Purge all the messy
Closets that reside
Inside your mind.

Become still.

You are safe.
You are home

GATHER
- Hyssop – 1 Tbsp. fresh or dried
- Kelp – 1 Tbsp. powder
- Salt
- Boiling water
- Tea infuser
- 2 large mugs
- Bathtub or small basin or large bowl

Hyssop is a powerful releasing herb on its own, but kelp takes this ritual to the next level. If the smell of kelp isn't your cup of tea, or you're not in the mood to rinse the kelp residue down the drain after your bath, feel free to omit it.

Place the kelp powder in one of your mugs and fill it with boiling water. Stir for about thirty seconds to help the kelp dissolve.

Fill a tea infuser with the hyssop, place it in your other

mug, then fill it with boiling water. Set a timer for fifteen minutes.

While your tub teas are steeping, draw a warm bath*. Toss some salt into your bathwater— whatever you have on hand is fine. When your potions have finished steeping, pour them both into your tub, and give it all a good counterclockwise swirl with your hands.

Step into the bath with the intention to release any bullshit weighing you down. You know what I'm talking about— that psychic sludge that doesn't belong to you and tells all the worst lies. The kind festering just below the surface that you didn't ask for, but that was foisted upon you anyway.

As you relax into the water, close your eyes and pay attention to how your body softens. Inhale into any areas of your body that need some extra love and attention, and exhale anything that feels drab and scratchy.

After a good soak, release your bathwater down the drain and imagine everything you expelled going down the drain with it.

Before you do anything else with your day, eat something that brings you comfort or joy. For extra potency, enjoy your food naked and proudly as the adoring air caresses your gorgeous animal body and dries you off.

*If you don't have access to a bathtub, use a small basin or the largest bowl you have to create a foot bath instead. Don't worry, the air wants to kiss your beautiful feet afterward.

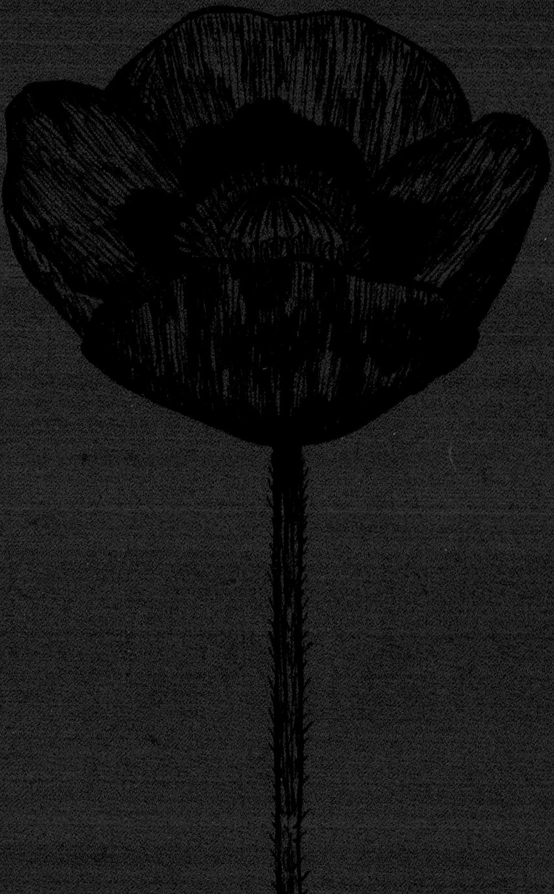

POPPY

Wield the sun
Like a beloved
Heirloom blanket.

Protected in
Generations of
Courage and
Worn threads.

Woven together
So long ago
To hold you in
This moment.

From this place
Of letting go
The next step
Is easy.

THE KID

It's okay to empty out or to feel a little emptied out because the inhale is coming. There is an expansion on the way.
—Chani Nicholas

August arrived with its bright white sunlight, and by the middle of the month, it shifted into a low golden descent into the outstretched liminal space between high summer and early fall. Nattie spent the previous two months graduating from community college, turning twenty-one, and touring university campuses. With a one-way ticket booked, her strong canary wings were primed to leave the nest and land in a dorm room 2,460 miles away.

In those weeks leading up to her departure, life rambled on in its ordinary way. We all went to work, took walks or bike rides in the morning before the asphalt became a hot cast iron skillet, folded our clean laundry, ate dinner together at our old wooden dining room table, and ran the dishwasher when it was full.

In the background, though, my mind kept drifting further and further backward until it landed on a memory from when Nattie was a six pound seven ounce newborn tucked into her car seat in the back of Mark's shitty black Volkswagen GTI that barely ran. I was sitting in the seat next to her while she held onto my right forefinger with her tiny pink baby hand. She looked up into my eyes as we passed by the old paper mill in Camas, and in that minuscule moment between new mother and new human, my mind wandered into the wide open spaces of the future.

Who will you become as you grow up, baby? I'm so excited to get to know you.

I can't even remember what those fantasies were in those early moments between us because who Nattie became is so much richer and more astounding than I could've ever imagined.

She's the kind of person who always catches the spiders and stinkbugs in our house and puts them outside.

And she's also the kind of person who breaks up with a boyfriend she really likes to go chase her dreams in college.

An aspiring drag king, she once spent a whole summer cutting and styling a long black wig so she could dress up as Dr. Ian Malcolm from *Jurassic Park* on Halloween.

She's smart as hell and has a voracious appetite for reading and learning. She loves to document her life in hand-illustrated comic strips.

She has an infectious laugh and can effortlessly crack up a whole room with her lightning quick one-liners.

She speaks up for what she believes in and knows expressing her truth and creativity is essential. She also knows how to listen and to keep her mind open and curious.

The pride, amazement, and love I felt for my kid swelled up inside me until it quietly leaked out of my eyes for weeks as I prepared to watch her go out into the big world on her own for the first time.

While she slowly packed up her room, miracles started dotting across my life like stars coming to life at dusk.

It all started one afternoon when a big blue heron flew low over our backyard while I was hanging up wet laundry on the line. She winked at me and dropped a folded piece of paper at my feet. I decided I'd read it later, so I went inside and placed it on the refrigerator door with a sturdy red magnet.

With steady and easy menstrual cycles, I finally got my post-ovulatory progesterone checked. It was low. My doctor recommended that when Ryan and I were ready to try for a baby again, I should take Clomid during the first few days of my cycle to help my follicles mature properly.

"That should create a corpus luteum that will create enough progesterone on its own," she explained, "But once you get a positive pregnancy test, I'll start monitoring your progesterone right away and prescribe you hormones if you still need them."

We had a plan, and we'd keep our fingers crossed from there.

"If it doesn't work out, we'll just get a dog," I told my hairdresser as I sat in her salon chair, the flowing black cape wrapped around my body.

She was behind me and stopped trimming my hair to look up at the big styling station mirror and into my eyes.

"You never know, maybe you and Ryan will get your rainbow baby now, and in two years, the perfect dog will find your family. That's what I hope happens for you guys," she said.

I smiled at her prayer.

"I hope so, too," I said, imbuing my own magic into the spell.

Ryan, who hadn't cut his hair since before our first miscarriage, told me one morning, "I think I'm finally ready for a haircut." He went to the barber that afternoon and asked the hairdresser to remove the two years of grief he'd been physically carrying on his shoulders.

"Oh yes, sweetie, let's get all this off you," she said, snapping the black cape around his neck, "It's time for a fresh start."

When he walked into the house with his handsome new 'do, he seemed lighter, and his eyes and smile beamed with renewed splendor.

I got a call from my dad a few days later. He found Nellie's old Kodak camera from 1915 buried in my parents' attic and wanted me to have it. I brought it home and set it on my dresser next to Mary's old radio. *For clear vision*, I thought.

The night Nattie flew the nest, we ate a huge celebratory sushi dinner at Takahashi on Holgate Boulevard. The unusually humid, cloudy weather matched the strangeness of those final moments before her departure. The hot, stale air clung to all our bodies, awaiting Nattie's big moment to fledge.

"I'm done packing," Nattie announced, leaving a pile of bubble wrap and old receipts on our living room floor as she wheeled her two big lime green suitcases toward the front door. Before we loaded them into the back of our car, I grabbed my garden shears off the back porch and clipped off four sprigs of horehound from the big bushy hedge filled with fragrant herbs along the chain-link fence in our front yard. I tucked two into each of Nattie's suitcases for protection and good luck.

During the previous few weeks, I imagined myself crying in the car all the way to the airport, but it didn't happen like that at all. The three of us just talked like it was a typical night. It wasn't until Nattie checked her bags and we all stood at the entrance to the airport terminal that tears began streaming down my cheeks.

I gently took her sweet face in my hands and said, "I'm so proud of you, kid. Seriously. So proud." And I gave her the biggest hug.

Then she turned to Ryan, and as he wrapped her up in his arms, he said gently, "I'm so proud of you, kid." His eyes were closed, and he was soaking up this moment. He didn't quite want to let her go yet.

When Nattie finally stepped back, her big blue eyes were a little shiny. She was sad to go, but her excitement for her first big adult adventure was shining through the most, and that made my heart even prouder. She gave us each another long hug and then started walking down the green carpeted hallway to get in line at the security checkpoint.

"There she goes," Ryan said softly as we watched her disappear.

I slipped my hand into his.

"How are you doing, Papa Bear?" I asked.

"You know, it's going to be so weird without her, and I'm going to miss her like crazy, but I'm excited for her. She's ready for this." He paused. "How are you doing, Mama?"

"At this moment, I'm just so proud of her, and I want all her dreams to come true," I wiped my eyes on the back of my hand and noticed the wise glowing orb in my center had calmly and sweetly encircled my heart.

Ryan nodded and squeezed my hand.

The next morning we woke up and wandered out into the living room naked, which felt new and exciting. We checked our phones and saw the texts Nattie had sent, letting us know she had made it safely. Sweet relief washed over us.

I walked into our little yellow kitchen, filled our electric kettle with water, and scooped peppermint green tea into the silver basket of the iron teapot. The cat meowed at my feet, rubbing her dark tiger stripes on my shins, buttering me up to serve her breakfast of kibble and canned meat.

Out of nowhere, I heard raindrops hitting our roof, so I made my way through the mudroom and opened the back door. A gush of refreshing cool wind wrapped itself around my body. I walked out into the backyard and felt the stiff, dry late-summer grass tickling the sides of my feet.

The rain started coming down harder, soaking my naked body as I stood in the grass with my arms stretched over my head. Each glittering drop was a different flower colored hue, creating a spectrum of flashy reds, bright yellows and oranges, deep purples, and soft greens all around me. I felt each one gently absorbing into my body.

I looked down and saw Wolf curled around my feet, looking up at me with her wise amber eyes. I smiled at her, then looked up into the silver clouds blanketed above me, taking in all the support from the unseen places.

When the rain let up, I walked back inside and dripped my way back to the kitchen. I took the basket of steeped tea leaves out of the teapot and looked up at the refrigerator door. In the cacophony of the previous weeks, I had forgotten about the note the great blue heron left for me.

I removed the big red magnet holding it in place and unfolded the creased paper in my hands.

More miracles are on the way.

ACKNOWLEDGMENTS

Huge waves of love and gratitude to my teacher, editor, and mentor, Ariel Gore. *Magic Flowers* was written mostly in workshops hosted in the Literary Kitchen and follows Gore's Grotto story structure. For classes, books and more info, visit **literarykitchen.net**.

Huge thanks also go out to the Wayward Writers, Jenny Forrester, Linda Rand, Jill Bradley, Kelsey Leigh, Sami Auclair, Laura McCullough DeLorme, Christopher Nemeth, Ryan Scott, Crystal Hanson, Tasia Stogianis, Al and Stewie Suh, Katy Simmons, Tina Cordes, Amy Rosko, Bob Potter, Patti Durovchic, Laurie Creager, Sue and Gene Blystone, Nancy Blystone, Aerial Brown, Nancy Dupuis, Paul Newson, Peter & Quincey Newson, Erin O'Neill, Polly Hatfield, Margaret Gervais, Amy Kimmick, Annie Cavanaugh, Sasha Konell, and all the incredible, generous folks who supported the Kickstarter campaign to bring this book to life.

I'd also like to acknowledge and thank the folks whose skills, expertise, and wisdom captured in books, classes, workshops, and mentorships have enriched my life with so much plant love and magic: Monika Lee, Richo Cech, Asia Suler, Scott Cunningham, Juliet Diaz, and Camilla Blossom Bishop.

To my husband, Ryan, and my daughter, Nattie—my love for you both soars past the boundaries of time and space. Thank you for all your love, excitement, support, and patience—and for believing in me, my writing, my voice, and this project. You both are my heart.

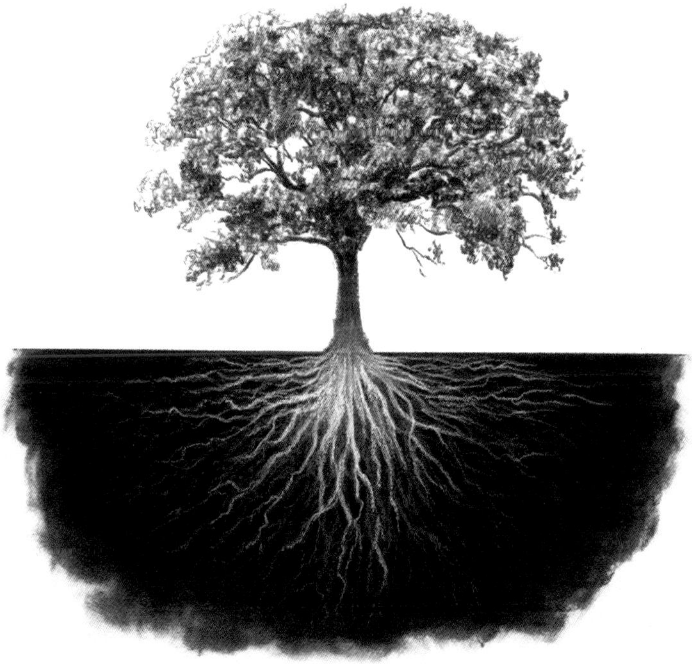

CHRISTINE BLYSTONE

is the creator and founder of Velvetback, where her work as a writer, artist, designer, and maker helps people connect with plants and make meaning with their magic. Her product line includes plant poetry oracle cards, botanical-infused bath salts, and natural incense cones. *Magic Flowers* is her debut novel.

Her work has a loyal fan base and has even reached luxury fashion designer Gabriella Hearst and Adventure Nannies founder Brandy Schultz. Velvetback products have been featured in Astral Box, Witchcraft Way and Writual Planner subscription boxes, received over 400 glowing 5-star reviews on Etsy, and are sold in brick-and-mortar shops worldwide.

She holds a bachelor's degree in graphic design from Portland State University, has studied Intuitive Plant Medicine with Asia Suler of One Willow Apothecaries, and continually hones her writing in workshops with author Ariel Gore.

velvetback.com • christine@velvetback.com